NEVER SAY DEAD

A RANDALL & CARVER MYSTERY

RANDALL & CARVER MYSTERIES
BOOK ONE

BLAIR HOWARD

Copyright © 2023 Blair Howard
Never Say Dead
All rights reserved.

No part of this publication may be reproduced, stored in a retrieval system, or transmitted in any form, or by any means, electronic, mechanical, photocopying, recording, or otherwise, without the express written permission of the publisher except for the use of brief quotations in a book review.

This novel is a work of fiction. The persons, places and events depicted in this novel were created by the author's imagination; no resemblance to actual persons, places or events is intended.

Product names, brands, and other trademarks referred to within this book are the property of the respective trademark holders. Unless otherwise specified, no association between the author and any trademark holder is expressed or implied. Nor does the use of such trademarks indicate an endorsement of the products, trademarks, or trademark holders unless so stated. Use of a term in this book should not be regarded as affecting the validity of any trademark, registered trademark, or service mark.

ISBN: 979-8-9876042-7-4

Library of Congress Control Number: 2023908919

Cleveland, TN, USA

For Jo, as always.

1

MONDAY EVENING

Mallory Carver leaned back against the bar counter and stared up at the water stains on the ceiling.

She didn't know how long they'd been there. She'd worked at The Saloon since... she specifically remembered the help wanted sign had appeared in October after she graduated high school, but she didn't apply until after Thanksgiving. And only then because she needed to get out of the house for a few hours each day. But the part-time job turned full-time, and...

Thirteen years later and I'm wondering if I can sell pictures of the ceiling for Rorschach tests, she thought.

She imagined a decade of drunks staring up at them, some seeing their mothers, others seeing their dogs. Maybe some saw a traumatic childhood event; *those would be the drunks that cried into their beer*, she thought.

She'd seen every kind of drunk you could imagine during her thirteen years at The Saloon.

Back in the day, when she was first hired, it had been

the Old West Saloon and Cattle Grill. It was a nice place then—fun music, good, inexpensive beer, an attractive menu, and even some coin-op horses out front for the kids to ride. Then the owner died, and it became Mustang Sally's. Sally kept the entire staff, which had been a relief, and she'd been a good boss and had treated everyone well. But then she'd had an emergency and moved out of state. After that it became the Quick Draw, an apt name since people didn't stay long when they found out how much the drinks cost. And now it was The Saloon, where the drinks were cheap because they were cheap drinks. The speaker system was old, dating from Sally's time, but she and the live music were long gone. And Vinnie, who'd owned the place for the last six years, cared more about the pennies he pinched than he did complaining customers.

It's a hole. And I can't dig my way out, she thought gloomily.

She looked at the clock. It was a little before nine PM—what once was peak hour—but the only customers she had was a booth full of bikers drinking the most tasteless domestic beer they had on tap, and Art Peters ensconced at the end of the bar with his sleep apnea.

"If we don't have any business, I guess I might as well start cleaning up," she muttered, slipping an earbud under her long blond hair and starting her favorite podcast.

She felt that familiar thrill at the clanking sound of the clock tower and the bong of the hour as Devin Rudd began his podcast. "Not every terrible tale begins with a terrible event. Many times, the most mundane happenings can lead to the most horrific murders. This, then, is the story of a man who wished to be an art student, and what his desires wrought for those around him. This, then, is another... *Dark Tiding.*"

As the music began, she wondered who it was going to

be this time. As Devin Rudd began to describe the idyllic setting in which the killer grew up, she stepped around the end of the bar, collected the bus bin and hauled it off to the dishwasher.

Where could she be? she wondered as she filled the dishwasher and pulled down the hatch. *It was just a routine hike.* As the water began sloshing around inside the washer, she tried to concentrate on the podcast. She'd missed the name of the killer—something mundane, someone she'd never heard of, which was unusual. She thought she knew them all; all those of any note, anyway.

The door buzzer jangled. She hurried back out to see who it was, but it was only the bikers leaving, a half-pitcher of warm beer on the table along with a ten-dollar bill. *At least I don't have to deal with them at closing time.*

Why hasn't she called her mom? It's been six days. Maybe she's lying hurt in a gully somewhere. She pushed the thought away. She had to work.

She grabbed another bus bin and walked over to clear the table, wrinkling her nose at the lingering smell of strong tobacco. *I don't mind the smell of tobacco, but that stuff reeks.* She waved a hand at the invisible odors, but they persisted. She hurriedly scraped the last of the paper trash into the bin and turned to flee the stink, but found herself facing Deputy Kal Cundiff.

"Evening, Mallory," Kal said.

She stopped, startled, the bus bin on her hip. Outside, the sound of motorcycles revving broke the silence.

"Oh, hi, Kal," she said, frowning. "I didn't hear you come in."

"That's because you're filling your ears with garbage," he said and smirked. "Who are you listening to tonight? Ed Gein? Ted Bundy? Or is it a five-part series on Charlie Manson?"

"It's not like that," she lied as she marched past him. But when she dropped the bin out back, she paused the podcast, slipped the bud out of her ear and into her pocket, and returned to her place behind the bar.

"All right," she said. "What brings you in here tonight? And in uniform? Don't tell me your dad has decided to take us seriously."

"Nah," Kal said and pulled a face, unable to look her in the eye. "The Sheriff's office has decided it doesn't qualify as a missing person's case."

"How can that be?" she insisted. "A person just has to be missing for more than forty-eight hours. Julie's been missing for *six days.*"

"Mal," he said plaintively, "this isn't one of those podcasts you listen to."

"Screw you, Kal," she snapped back. "Julie is a responsible young woman. She's an experienced hunting guide. She knows the trails like the back of her hand. Ever since Jared got hurt, she's been the dependable rock of the family. She wouldn't just... fly off and disappear without telling someone. It's not in her nature."

"Well, you know... sometimes the pressure builds up," Kal said in his best TV-cop voice. "All that responsibility, helping to run the business and all. And she decides to up and take a crazy vacation. It happens all the time. She'll be back. Mal, we never found her car, not at any of the trailheads. Not everything is some stupid criminal murder conspiracy."

"Is that what you think of me, Kal Cundiff? You think I'm bitching about my missing niece because I listened to a story?" She stepped around the end of the bar and stopped in front of him, using every inch of her five-foot-ten to loom over him. "My sister, Jennifer," she continued, "and my entire family is halfway to mourning because they think she might be lying dead up there in the forest somewhere, and all you can do is make sick remarks."

"Look, Mal, I'm sorry," Kal said, his face turning a rosy hue.

Mallory stepped back behind the bar and slammed down the hatch with a bang.

"Really?" she snapped. "You're sorry. Your dad is sorry. And my sister is at home crying over her missing daughter, and your department doesn't seem to care at all. Was there any other reason you stopped by to see me? If not, I have to close up, so you need to leave."

Kal reached around and pulled out a notebook from his hip pocket. "Okay. I was out of line, and I apologize. As it happens, I'm here to get a few details. Since you fancy yourself an amateur detective, you probably have them all memorized, right?"

She wanted to glare at him, slap the mocking smile off his face, but there was a sliver of hope: *Is he finally going to take it seriously?*

"Where do you want me to start?" she asked.

"You can gimme the basics first," he replied, his pen poised.

"Her name is Julie Romero. She's twenty-three, five-eight, slim, one-hundred-twenty-two pounds, with blonde, shoulder-length hair. She had her dog, Tobin, with her. Her parents have lived in Chattanooga for the last forty-four years. My sister, Jennifer, her mother, told me that she left last Tuesday morning for a hike on Red Grove Trail, off Highway 64; she didn't know which branch."

"Yeah, I heard," he said. "Red Grove. She oughta know better than to go into the forest up there by herself."

"And why not?" she asked, giving him an annoyed glare. "She's an experienced guide."

She knew that many of the locals had some wild ideas

about the mountains and the Cherokee National Forest. And, while there were plenty of real-life dangers associated with walking through forests and mountains, centuries of Native American folklore and campfire stories had convinced half the population that the place was crawling with eldritch deities, dark forces commanded by witches, ghosts, territorial moonshiners, and cannabis and mandrake farmers. Most of it was bunk as far as she was concerned, but Kal didn't look too eager to check out the forbidding forest.

"Look, Julie isn't just some hiker," she said. "She's an experienced hunting guide. She works for her dad, Jared Romero, at his big hunting outlet off 64. She doesn't just get lost in her own backyard."

"Experienced hikers can and do get lost," Kal argued. "Happens all the time."

"Not Julie," she snapped. "If she was going to be late back, she'd have texted her father. What about her Bronco? That wouldn't just get lost, too, would it?"

"We've had an APB out for almost a week," Kal replied. "If nobody's found it, it means it's left the county. And with no evidence to the contrary, it looks like she drove it away."

Mallory opened her mouth to speak, but Kal beat her to it.

"Let me ask you something, Mal. Do you want to be here? In Chattanooga?"

Mallory paused.

"Because you just said she's lived here basically her whole life," he continued. "She's never been anywhere else. Never seen the big cities. Never tasted life outside of town or even outside her own family. How happy was she working for her dad?"

Mallory knew that Julie was frustrated with her dad at

times. But she always smiled at everything... but was there pain behind that smile? Longing? Frustration?

How long had Mallory wanted to just pack up and leave? When exactly had *she* decided to stay? She had a sharp mind and a good education, with a 4.0 grade point average. Why did she stay? Why would Julie stay? *Because it's home. That's why.*

"See?" Kal said righteously when she didn't reply. "I knew you'd understand. Just give her another week and she'll come rolling back into town, apologize for being so thoughtless, and then brag about her big adventure in Nashville."

A part of Mallory wanted to believe him. It was an easy out, and it fulfilled all the criteria: Julie was safe. She was having a little reckless fun. Everything would be fine.

But it didn't answer the real questions, the ones her family kept asking. *Why* did she? *How* could she? *Where* is she? Why hasn't she called? And why is her phone off?

"We're not going to agree on this, Kal," Mallory said sadly. "I guess we just don't understand each other. It isn't personal. No one will listen to us, so Jennifer is going to do something about it herself."

Kal looked alarmed. "You don't mean she's going to go trekking up there her own self? That's insane. She does that, we'll have a real missing person's case on our hands."

"No, she's not going to do that. She's not stupid, Kal. She said she's going into the city tomorrow. Though, I suppose she might have lied to us and planned to run away into the woods instead."

"What's she gonna do, then?" Kal demanded.

"She's going to hire Tucker Randall," Mallory said.

"*What?* That overpriced PI who takes on, what, three or four cases a year? Your family is seriously going to put trust in that hack?"

"We haven't been seeing any results from your department so far, have we?" Mallory said.

"Tucker Randall is a publicity hound," Kal replied. "He'll suck you dry and leave you looking stupid while he parades around on TV."

"Better stupid than useless." Mallory saw that her jibe had hit its mark.

"Well, I've got to get going," Kal said and stuffed the notepad back in his pocket.

"Get it all down, did you?" Mallory asked, smirking, knowing he hadn't written a word.

Kal rolled his shoulders, adjusted his belt, looked at her and said, "Good luck with Randall, but I ain't holding my breath." As he opened the door, he threw one last shot. "If he even takes the case, which I sincerely doubt he will."

Mallory resisted the urge to throw something at the door. Instead, she stomped to the other end of the bar and gave Art a little shove. "Come on, Art. It's closing time. Do I need to call your brother?"

"What?" Art looked at her, then scrunched up his face as he tried to focus. "Nah-uh-uh. I'm good. I'll get home just fine."

I hope Julie gets home just fine, too.

2

TUESDAY MORNING 9AM

It was just before nine and a beautiful morning, though Tucker Randall ignored the sunlight streaming in through slats in the window blinds as he studied the open manila folders spread across his desk. His eyes flickered over forensic photos and police reports, but the file he was most interested in was the Nebraska case, the one he was tapping with the fingertips of his left hand. He was pretty certain it would be the most interesting of the six cases, but he wanted to make his decision with more than just a hunch and a fee.

He turned his attention to the case in Jacksonville, Oklahoma. *If I take this one, Nate will start bugging me to visit his kids again...*

The door opened, and his assistant poked her head inside and said, "Mr. Randall?"

"What is it, Debbie?" he asked, hoping she wasn't feeling chatty.

"You have a call on line one. It's your brother."

"Speak his name, and he shall appear," he muttered as he picked up the phone. "Nate," he said. "How's my favorite brother?"

"Your only brother. At least that's what Mom says," Nate replied.

"You know," Tucker said. "Technically, I'm not open yet. So I'm going to add an inconvenience charge to your bill, and—"

"Haha. Very funny," Nate replied. "I figured you'd still be in bed. I figured you'd be jet-lagged?"

"Nate, it was LA, not India. I lose more sleep than that on an average night."

"See, Tucker, this is what I'm talking about. You just throw yourself into these things with no regard for your health. Take a week off. Come out here to Tulsa. It's Ella's birthday on Saturday, and Laura's making a strawberry cake. The kids would love to see you."

"While I do enjoy Laura's cooking," Tucker replied, "I don't think I'll have time." He picked up the Jacksonville file and set it aside. "Besides, you're the family man, not me."

"You can say that again. Mom's losing hope on that one." Nate sighed—and a crackle of static burst in Tucker's ear. "So you won't come to Ella's party?"

"I'll be in Nebraska," Tucker replied. "It has everything I like in a case, and they still have snow up there."

"Why do you do this to yourself?" Nate asked, exasperated.

"Obviously, because I like it. Otherwise, I wouldn't," Tucker replied. "What are you talking about, exactly?"

"Your MO. This thing you have about taking only one case at a time. I'm a cop, and you and I both know it can take months to close a case. You're limiting yourself,

CHAPTER 2　　　　　　　　　　　　　　　　　　　　　15

Tucker, and you know you have more to offer, no matter whose hat you're wearing."

"I don't wear hats." Tucker paused. He could hear voices in the next room. Debbie was talking to someone. *A client? Arguing? No, two clients. Why are they raising their voices?*

"Tucker? You still there?" Nate asked.

"Yeah, I'm here. Just hold on a sec. Someone's in the outer office."

The arguing in the other room continued. *What the hell?*

His door opened, and two people burst in, a man and a woman.

"Tucker? Is this still about Marsha?"

"Sorry, Nate. I have to go. Clients. I'll call you later, okay?" And he hung up the phone before Nate could dredge up the past, again.

Whoever they are, they have a cosmic sense of timing.

"I'm sorry, Mr. Randall," Debbie said, flustered. "I tried to tell them you're not accepting new clients, but they wouldn't listen. They shoved past me. Do you want me to call the police?"

"No. Please don't call the police," the woman said, obviously distressed. "If you'll just hear us out. Give us five minutes, and then we'll leave. I promise."

He stood and looked at the couple. The first thing he realized was that the man was taller than he was. He had to be at least six-four. He towered over poor Debbie.

But that wasn't all. They both had that desperate look in their eyes, and there was also something about the woman. Something he couldn't quite place. She looked familiar. *I've seen her somewhere before, but where?*

"Please, have a seat," he said. "Thank you, Debbie. I don't think we'll need the police."

"I'm really sorry," the woman said as she sat down. "We're not normally this pushy. I mean, I've never—"

"There's no need to apologize," Tucker said. "Tell me about your problem, and I'll tell you if I can help."

She nodded, took a deep breath, and began, "I'm Jennifer Romero, and this is my husband, Jared. Our daughter, Julie, is missing. She went hiking, and she didn't return. We're hoping you can find her."

"Your daughter," Tucker said. "Is she an experienced hiker?"

"She's experienced," Jared said. "She works for me as a hunting and fishing guide. She knows the forest better than anyone I know. I own Romero's Outdoors out on 64, as you probably know. She's been hiking the trails since I carried her on my back when she was a kid."

By then, Tucker was only half listening to them. It was a missing person case, and he hated those. He'd spent more time during his years in the FBI chasing wayward kids than he cared to remember, and he was already regretting agreeing to listen to them.

In his mind, he was already setting up shop in a cabin in Northern Nebraska. He could smell the rich scent of crackling pine in the fireplace and taste the heat of strong black coffee on a cold morning.

He made a mental note to ask Debbie to check for the next available flight as he listened to Jared drone on about his daughter. Tucker told himself that as soon as they were done talking, he'd politely decline their business and refer them to another private investigator, but then he caught something Jennifer said that jerked him out of his reverie.

"...she went out to hike one of the trails, one that she's walked a hundred times, but she never came back. She didn't call. Her phone goes straight to voicemail. And her Bronco's disappeared. So has her dog, Tobin."

I could pitch this one to Billy, he thought. *He's nice, and he won't cheat them when the girl turns up in another day or two.*

CHAPTER 2

"...and it's been a week now with no word."

"Wait," Tucker said. "A week? Why haven't you gone to the Sheriff's department? I'm just a private eye. They have far more resources than I do."

"We did," she said. "We filed a report, but they won't do anything. They won't even listen to us. They say there's no evidence and that she's probably just taken off for a few days."

He stared at her.

"They should be looking for her," Jennifer continued. "They really should, shouldn't they? But they aren't, and why would they? There are a lot of missing person cases in and around Chattanooga. It's a big city, and there are so many hiking trails around here, especially in the forests, and that just makes it worse. I guess they don't have time to investigate them all."

She was, he knew, referring to the Cherokee and Prentice Cooper forests, and many smaller ones besides. And he grimaced as he thought of the folklore and mystery that surrounded them, especially the Cherokee National Forest. It's vast, more than seven-hundred-thousand acres vast. Plenty of people had gone missing in the forest, never to be seen or heard from again.

"Exactly," Jared said. "I've talked to the county sheriff's office, several times, and the local police department. They won't even listen to us. They won't even acknowledge that she's missing."

Tucker raised an eyebrow and decided to play devil's advocate. "They could be right, you know."

Jennifer Romero stood up, slammed her hands down on the desk in front of him, leaned in and looked him in the eyes. And again, he was sure he'd seen her somewhere before.

"Julie would *never* leave," she said angrily. "Never! I

know it. My husband knows it, and my sisters know it. All our friends know it. You have to believe us."

"We know something's wrong," Jared said quietly. "As Jen said, her phone goes straight to voicemail, and there's also been no activity on her bank account or her credit cards."

"You have access to her bank account?" Tucker asked.

"Yes. If she'd 'taken a vacation,' she'd need money, wouldn't she?"

"It was Mallory's idea," Jared said. "She's Jen's sister. She's a bit of a true-crime buff. She listens to podcasts about it all the time. Anyway, she insisted, so we keep all the important stuff, passwords, bank accounts and such in a folder."

A true crime nut. That's all I need, Tucker thought, resisting the urge to shake his head. It was a missing person case. He didn't do missing persons, and the mention of a possible amateur detective wanna-be drove the final nail into the proverbial coffin. So he dusted off the script he'd memorized for just such a situation.

"I'm really sorry," he began. "I understand how you feel, but I already have several commitments. And I just don't have the time to take on a new client. I can, however, refer you to my colleague, Will Preston. He is an excellent investigator, and he'll be happy to..."

He trailed off as Jennifer pushed a photo across the desk and said, "Look at her. It's my daughter, Julie. Look at her and tell me she's run away. Do it."

So he looked, and his breath caught in his throat. The photograph had been cropped, but the girl's face was a face from the past, a face that haunted his dreams. *Marsha! Marsha Cline?*

CHAPTER 2

SIC David Lewis was seated at his desk, leaning back in his chair, his fingers steepled in front of him.

"Agent Randall... Tucker," he said, "I know this wasn't supposed to happen—"

"I did exactly what you told me to, David," Tucker said, interrupting him. "It was a done deal, you said. Marsha Cline's going to make it happen, you said. And all I had to do was to persuade her to make a statement. Which I did. She trusted me, David. You were supposed to protect her."

"There was an unforeseen—"

"Why, David?" Tucker shouted, leaning forward in his chair. "We're the Federal Bureau of Investigation, for God's sake."

"For what it's worth, Tucker, I really am sorry." He slid a glass across the desk. "Here. Have something."

Tucker took the glass, raised it to his lips, and felt the sting on his split lip where Lisa Cline had punched him in the mouth for breaking his promise to protect her daughter.

"You son of a bitch," he said, staring David in the eye and slowly shaking his head. "You had no intention—"

"It's not your fault, Tucker," David said easily. "It's not anybody's fault."

Tucker stood up, took a step forward and slammed the glass down on the desktop. It shattered with a sound like a gunshot.

The gunshot that had ended Marsha Cline's life.

He looked down at the scar in the palm of his hand. *If Marsha Cline had never met me, she'd still be alive,* he thought, then looked at the photo again. The resemblance was startling.

Julie Romero. Her eyes had that same overflowing joy for life as Marsha's once did. Her hair was a shade or two darker; her eyes were brown, while Marsha's were green.

She was tanned, and there was a constellation of freckles spread across her smiling face.

Tucker could also see the resemblance in Jennifer Romero, and it pained him to look at her. If Marsha had been granted the chance to grow older, have a family, and live life to the full, Tucker was sure she'd look a lot like Jennifer.

He looked at her, nodded, sighed and said, "All right, I'll do it. I'll take your case."

"Oh, God. Thank you! Thank you."

And, as he looked into her eyes, glistening with tears, he wondered what the hell kind of a mess he'd just stepped into.

3

TUESDAY 5PM

Mallory removed yet another stack of papers from her home printer. This last batch was streaky, and she made a mental note to pick up more ink at Staples the following morning.

She thumbed through them, making sure she'd printed everything, then carefully placed the stack into a manila folder labeled "recent correspondences."

In anticipation of her meeting with Tucker Randall, she'd compiled as much information as she could. She'd spoken with everyone she knew who had contact with Julie and asked them to send her screenshots of their last text conversations. In addition, she'd marked Julie's usual hiking trails on a map and cross-referenced those areas with other missing persons cases she'd found in the news.

Mallory wasn't sure how much of this information was essential, but she figured every little bit counted. She was just sliding the folders into her messenger bag when her phone rang.

"Hey," Jennifer said. "We just got here. Are you on your way?"

"I'm leaving now. I'll be there in about twenty minutes. Is the PI there yet?"

"Not yet," Jennifer said. "We just got here. He isn't supposed to be here until five, and it's only... four-twenty-five. We'll go ahead and ask for a table in the back. I'll order coffee. See you soon, okay?"

Mallory said her goodbyes and then headed out to her car. Usually, she listened to the radio while she drove, but today she coasted along the back roads in silence, glancing now and again at the distant mountains.

The trail Julie was supposed to have taken was some forty-five minutes east of Collegedale, where she lived, off Highway 64, and Mallory couldn't help but imagine her niece up there somewhere, beyond the tree line, lying in a gully with a broken leg. *But where the hell is her Bronco? And why is her phone off?*

"We'll find you, Julie," she said under her breath. "I promise." And she prayed her obsession with true crime and mysteries would, just for once, come in handy. She hoped the vast amount of information she'd managed to compile would assist the PI and that he would find Julie as soon as possible. She was also aware, however, that much of what she had gathered was hearsay.

But maybe, she thought, *just maybe, it will help paint a more accurate picture of Julie's character and give him some insight as to what could have happened to her.*

It was ten minutes to five when she pulled into the parking lot at the Mountainside Café that afternoon. She parked as close to the entrance as possible, grabbed her messenger bag, opened the door, stepped out and closed and locked it behind her.

She looked around the parking lot, noting the preponderance of pickup trucks, shook her head and stepped inside, wondering why Jen had insisted on holding the meeting way out there.

Like many such places in the area—and there were quite a few, all of them dependent upon the seasonal outdoor population for their livelihood—the café had seen better days. The log exterior begged to be refurbished. The planters outside the front entrance lacked attention, and weeds filled the gutters. *Life always finds a way,* she thought as she pushed through the pair of foyer doors and into the restaurant.

Mallory could remember going there as a child, barely old enough to go to school. Jennifer was getting ready to graduate high school, and Katie had already met and was dating her husband-to-be. They would stop by for lunch after church most weeks. But it had been years since Mallory had last eaten there, and somehow, she felt a similar melancholy for the run-down restaurant as she did for The Saloon. Time had weathered both almost beyond recognition.

Julie, she thought as she pushed through the first set of doors into the foyer. As the youngest sibling, Mallory had taken to Jennifer's new baby. Eagerly, she'd taken on the role of big sister, and she stayed close to her through the years, mentoring her, supporting her, and showing her how to do... practically everything.

She pushed through the second set of doors, paused just inside, looked around and spotted her sister waving from a booth at the back.

"Hey, big sis, big bro," she said as she slid into the seat opposite them. "Any sign of Mr. Randall yet?"

"I got a text from him a few minutes ago," Jennifer said. "He's on his way. He should be here shortly."

"Good," Mallory said and dumped a folder on the table. "We have a few minutes to go over these, then."

"What's all that, Mallory?" Jennifer asked.

"A little bit of everything," Mallory replied as she rifled through the papers. "Just the most pertinent stuff to start with. I have copies of her emails, text messages and her last bank statement. I also have statements I took from some of her closest friends, you know, like Sarah and Jane, and compiled those as well. And these." She opened the manila folder labeled "Maps" and pushed it toward Jared.

"Do you mind looking those over to make sure I mapped out Julie's usual routes correctly? I used the info from your company website and also from Julie's personal notes, but I want to make sure I haven't missed anything."

Jennifer flipped through a few of the files, barely glancing at the contents. "How'd you get access to all this?"

"The family folder gave me a lot of what I needed, but I made some phone calls and went out and pounded the pavement a little."

"You pounded the pavement?" Jennifer scrunched up her face in disbelief. "Mallory, you sound like some kind of off-beat TV detective. The next thing you'll be telling us is that you canvassed the neighborhood or grilled some suspects. Please try to act like a normal person when Mr. Randall gets here."

Mallory pulled a face but smiled and shook her head. Jennifer had long since adopted the role as her second mother, which only got worse after their mother passed away. Regardless of Jennifer's good intentions, it sometimes got a little old.

Just once, I wish she'd give me a little credit, she thought, but then she took those feelings and pushed them aside. *Today is about Julie.*

"There he is," Jennifer said and waved.

Mallory turned and looked at him. He was tall. At least six-one. Well-built with brown hair.

"So that's him, is it?" Mallory said, unable to hide the fact that she was impressed.

Randall walked confidently across the restaurant toward them, weaving his way through the afternoon crowd.

"Mal, come and sit over here so we can all talk to him," Jennifer said.

"Oh, right, yes, of course," she stuttered as she scooped up the papers and stuffed them back into the folder, fumbling it so that it fell to the floor, spilling its contents.

Stupid, stupid, stupid, she scolded herself as she knelt to gather the wayward file.

"Here, let me help you," he said, bending down beside her.

"So you must be Mallory?" he asked quietly, as he helped her gather the contents of the file. "Jennifer told me about you. She said you were… organized, and I see that you are."

"O-o-oh. Um, thank you," Mallory said as she carefully stood up and sat down next to her sister.

Oh, for Pete's sake, just let me get through this without embarrassing myself even more.

"This looks… impressive and… thorough," Randall said, staring at the folder.

"This is my sister, Mallory Carver," Jennifer said. "And she is all about thorough. Ouch." Mallory had kicked her ankle.

"Hello, Mr. Randall," Mallory said sweetly, glancing at her sister. "I've put together some information I think you'll find helpful."

"Wow," Randall said as he flipped through the pages.

"Well, Miss Carver, the more information I have, the better. Thank you."

"You're welcome," Mallory replied, and eager to prove that she wasn't an incompetent idiot, she took four more folders from her messenger bag and dumped them on the table in front of him. "That one you have there is just the summary folder. I have everything sorted and indexed in these."

4

TUESDAY 5:30PM

When Tucker pulled into the Mountainside Café parking lot, he couldn't help but notice the dilapidated state of the building. *How can the owners let the place go like this?* he wondered. *Surely it can't be that hard to keep up with the routine maintenance.*

In the back of his mind, he could hear something his supervisor David once said to him. He couldn't remember the words exactly, but it was something about getting up every day, getting dressed, and then you realize that's all you have the energy for and that you're just going through the motions to get through the day.

Is that what you were doing with Marsha, David? Just going through the motions, damn you.

He couldn't understand how someone could become so hidebound as to miss the obvious on the way to the mundane, but he himself hadn't reached that stage yet. He still had time to ponder the secrets of life before they caught up with him.

He walked into the restaurant and spotted Jennifer Romero waving at him. She was with her husband and a blonde woman sitting opposite them. Jennifer said something to her and she rose to her feet, dropping a folder full of papers on the floor.

"Here, let me help," he offered and crouched down beside her. She turned her head to look at him, and he was astonished to see that she didn't look like her sister at all. This woman was… lovely, not that Jennifer wasn't. She was. But Mallory, if that's who she was, was different. She was taller than her sister, with large hazel eyes, and she looked fit as if she worked out.

The papers were now back in the folder, and she grabbed it from him and quickly scooted into the seat opposite him, close to her sister.

Tucker frowned to himself, thinking there must be quite an age gap between them.

Mallory said hello and handed him the file, saying something about helpful information.

He took it from her, opened it and flipped through the papers. *Sheesh,* he thought. *This is exactly what I expected. Reams of paper. Every kind of document imaginable.*

The folder also contained several trail maps, a dozen or more pages of texts and emails with highlights and handwritten notations, usually saying something like "Clearly not going on vacation" next to someone's text about what Julie was doing "next week," trail safety statistics with one dating back to 1975. Prevalence of animal attacks, broken down by category. There were even customer satisfaction ratings for the boots the girl was wearing and a recent doctor's physical for Julie.

"Wow," he said, trying not to sound condescending, and something to the effect that the more information he had, the better.

CHAPTER 4

"You're welcome," she said and dumped four more files on the table in front of him.

He stared at the pile of paperwork for a moment, then looked up at her to say something about overreach, but he saw that she was watching him intently.

At first, because of the dropped folder, he'd assumed she was an easily flustered klutz. But suddenly, he wasn't so sure. Her jaw was jutted, her face set, and there was a formidable look of... a mixture of anger, confidence, vulnerability and even determination. This, he realized, was probably a girl who was told every day that she wasn't good enough, that she was wasting her time and energy. *Maybe*, he mused, *her family, and her sister in particular, gave her a hard time about her fascination with true crime, just as I did, even before I met her. But,* he thought with an inward sigh, *who listens to those things? People who want to be me. And who the hell would want to be me? If only they knew.*

He stared at the exhaustive stack of research, then looked at Mallory, smiled and said, "Thank you again." Thinking, *even if most of it is likely useless.*

"So, Mallory, what do you do for a living?" he asked as he flipped from one page to the next. "Do you work with Julie at the outlet?"

"No, I'm a bartender," she said in a challenging tone of voice. "And I have been for thirteen years."

He looked at her and nodded. She was tanned, but she didn't have the outdoorsy complexion her sister and brother-in-law shared. He also realized that he'd mistaken her age as well. Maybe it was just Julie on his mind, but he'd pegged her to be in her mid-twenties. But with thirteen years behind a bar, she had to be more than thirty. Not that he was going to ask her—being an investigator didn't remove as many social graces as one might think.

That's what background checks are for, he thought, inwardly smiling to himself.

"And where do you work?" he asked, flipping through the pages.

"You probably passed it on the way here," she said, "It's… The Saloon."

Oh, that place? He recalled the shabby building. *Geez, if the Mountainside Café needs a refurbish, The Saloon needs... well, never mind. And this...* He gazed at the collection of pages of emails, text messages and colorful emojis. *None of it makes any sense.* There were actual words here and there, including one that caught his eye, "Can't wait until Music Fest next month," but the rest…

"Those are from Julie's best friend, Sarah Alexander," Mallory said. "They've been friends since middle school. They go everywhere together, and they tell each other everything. That file contains all of Julie's text conversations from the past month."

"Yes, yes. This should all be very enlightening," Tucker lied. "You must have worked very hard to put all of this…" *Whew, wow.* "…valuable information together. But I think it'll be better if I go over it alone, at my office. There are too many distractions here for me to do it justice." And he began to gather the paperwork.

"Oh, I completely understand," Jennifer said.

"But what if you have questions?" Mallory said. "I can help."

Tucker made a point not to look at her as he turned toward the Romeros. "I can always call you if something comes up, can't I?"

"Yes, of course," Jennifer replied. "Anytime."

"You have both of our cell numbers," Jared said. "Please don't hesitate to call."

Mallory frowned, not quite believing what was happening.

"Now," Tucker said as he stood up, throwing back his half-full mug of coffee as if it had been a shot. "I've got to get going. There's a lot for me to go through." He hefted the stack of folders and smiled. "I'll reach out to you as soon as I know something." Again, he spoke only to the Romeros. "And please, call me if you think of anything that might be helpful."

"But," Mallory said, "I could help."

"I'll keep that in mind," Tucker said, smiling politely. "It was nice to meet you, Mallory." Then he turned again to the Romeros and said, "I'm going to head back to my office now. If you need me, you know where to find me."

And with that, he wished them all a good evening and left, thinking he had a much better understanding of Jennifer's younger, true crime fanatic sister.

The entire meeting had lasted less than thirty minutes, and he was glad to be out of there, once again wondering what the hell he'd gotten himself into.

5

TUESDAY EVENING 7:30PM

"Can you believe it?" Mallory asked for the third time. "The nerve of that guy."

"Some nerve," Vinnie agreed.

"He completely shut me out! It was like I wasn't even there. Where does he get off doing that? Do you think he'll even bother to look at my files?"

She whipped her head around to look at her boss, Vinnie Mars. "I mean, he will, right? I put a lot of hours into them."

Her employer, the elderly man with the liver spots on his tanned bald head, was kneeling on the floor on the other side of the bar, tightening the screws at the base of one of the circular barstools.

"I would hope so," Vinnie replied, not bothering to look up at her.

"I know, right?" Mallory agreed. "I've spent the whole week compiling all that information. There's a lot of it. Sure, but some of it's got to be important, doesn't it?'

"Uh-huh," Vinnie responded.

"Of course it is," she said. "I mean, I mapped out Julie's hiking trails, didn't I? That should be useful, right? I worked really hard on that, making sure it was all laid out accurately, which was difficult because the Red Grove trail isn't even on some of the maps."

"Yeah," Vinnie responded.

"If that dumb PI doesn't even look through the files... You know, I probably would have been better off going to the police. Maybe I shouldn't have been so quick to dismiss Kal. If I'd have pressed him hard enough, I bet I could have made him listen to me."

"Probably," the old man mumbled, his shaking hands struggling to align the screwdriver with the slot.

"Now all that information is lost," she said. "Gone! It's all gone! I should have made a copy, but I didn't. Why was I so stupid to think Tucker Randall would listen to me? Nobody ever listens to me."

"Yeah, that's not good," Vinnie's lackluster voice intoned.

Mallory frowned at her boss. "Vinnie. Are *you* even listening to me?"

"Sounds good," he responded.

Her frown deepened, but she continued to talk. "You know, sir. I think I'll set fire to the place, starting with the contents of the office safe. What d'you think about that?"

"You know best," the man replied. His tongue was stuck out as he twisted the screwdriver.

Upset that she was once again being ignored, Mallory slammed the aluminum shaker she'd been cleaning down on the bar. The noise reverberated through the room, attracting the attention of just about everyone in the room.

"Is something wrong, Mallory?" Vinnie asked, squinting up at her through his steel-framed glasses.

CHAPTER 5

"Oh, no. Nothing at all," Mallory said sarcastically. "Julie's missing. I've lost a whole week's work, and nobody ever listens to me."

Vinnie stood up and arched his back. "Ooh, that's... ow. My back! I need to go see a chiropractor," he complained, but after a few seconds, he looked at her and said, "So what're you going to do about it, then?"

Mallory sighed and rolled her eyes. "You know," she said thoughtfully. "I can't even start over. Not only was I stupid not to make copies, but I also gave Tucker all the login information. Why did I do that?"

"You want to know what I think?" Vinnie wheezed, holding his back. "I think you should take it as a sign, right?"

"How so?" she asked, hoping that maybe, just *maybe*, he had some advice to offer.

"A sign that you should get on with your job and let that city-slicker do his. That's what I think."

Mallory stared at him for a moment, then sighed and said, "Whatever you say, sir."

"Atta girl," he mumbled. "I gotta go sit down. M'back's killing me," he said as he stepped carefully around the bar and patted her shoulder. "You worry too much, my dear. I'm sure your niece is fine." He squeezed her shoulder and, with a hand on his back and the other sliding along the bar top, he walked slowly back to his office.

She heaved a sigh, grabbed her cloth and went to work on the rings on the bar top.

Damn it, she thought. *Why doesn't anybody ever listen to me? Not even Vinnie. Whew. Geez. I don't get it. Tucker Randall was supposed to fix everything. I gave him all that information, and he wouldn't even look at me. What is wrong with me? Why does he treat me like that? I hate this frickin' place. I've been stuck here ever since Mom died. I lost my scholarship to UTK...*

everything, and all because I was the only one who stepped up when she got ill. Me! No one else. And now they all treat me like I'm a moron. And now Julie. And this... this... Tucker Randall.

"Hey, Mal. You gonna take the varnish right off."

Mallory jerked her head up to find Howie O'Neal standing at the bar with an empty glass in his hand.

"Oh, hey, Howie. Yeah, I have a lot on my mind. You need a refill?"

He shook his head. "Nah. It's about time for me to head on home. I just wanted a quick word with you before I go."

"Okay. What's up?" Mallory asked.

"Well," he began apprehensively, "I didn't mean to eavesdrop on y'all, but this place is awful quiet, and I caught the last part of your conversation with Vin about your cousin."

"Niece. Julie's my niece," she said.

"Right, right," Howie said. "Sorry. Did I hear you say somethin' about the girl being up near Red Grove when she went missing?"

Mallory nodded slowly. "Uh-huh. Yes, why?"

"Well. I'm sure y'already know I'm a bit of a mountain man m'self. Back before Jared's injury, we used to go huntin' up that way, two or three times a year; turkey and boar, up toward Banner Road. 'Course, that was a long time ago... Is that where she went?"

"Yes. Yes, it is," Mallory said. "She hikes up there all the time."

"Huh!" Howie pulled a face. "Ain't no good no more." He glanced at Mallory, frowning. "There's some unsavory characters up yonder. Squatters and 'shiners. Even wood witches, so some folk say."

"Are you saying Julie was kidnapped by moonshiners or witches?"

"What? No. 'Course not. But there's a little cabin out

there. No one goes near it no more. They say the Burns boy is squattin' there."

"Burns... you mean Zach Burns? I thought he left town years ago."

"Yeah. Him," Howie said. "No. He still lives up there in the cabin. You know, I saw him take a deer with a bow once," Howie continued. "Big un it was... durndest thing I ever did see. Hell of a shot, so it was."

"You don't think he could have anything to do with Julie being missing, do you?"

Howie shrugged, pulled a face and said, "We've never had no trouble with him. Truth be told, I've only encountered him a handful of times. And he was just about as nice as you could want."

Mallory bit her fingernail as she considered this alarming new twist.

"Still," she muttered, staring down at Howie's empty glass.

"Yeah," Howie said, "I can't help but think about his poor mom, Wynona. He was only seventeen when he killed her. How could a kid like that kill his own mother? If he could do that as a boy, who knows what he's capable of doing now? Especially to a pretty young girl like Julie."

"He was never convicted, though, was he?" she said.

"Well, no," Howie replied. "I s'pose not. But I reckon everyone knows he done it. He was... what do they call it on TV? The prime suspect, the only suspect, really."

That's true, Mallory thought, then said, "As I remember it, there was no direct evidence. What they did have was all circumstantial, so they dropped the charges."

"Yeah, but the boy had injuries, didn't he?" Howie said. "He said he'd been fighting to save his mom but couldn't tell anyone who with or how he got 'em. I don't know how he got away scot-free like he did. Everyone in town knows he must have gotten those injuries from fightin' with his mom. It's hard to believe the cops and the judge believed all that blackout BS he was spouting."

"disassociative amnesia," Mallory said, nodding. *But if he did kill her, and if he's out there...*

"Anyway," Howie said, "just thought I'd mention it. Try not to worry about it. After all, it could've been one of the wood witches or 'shiners who nabbed her up. I'm off 'ome now. See you tomorrow."

"Thank you, Howie," she called over her shoulder as he walked out the door.

She turned her attention to the register, her head full of thoughts of Zach Burns. She'd known him in high school, sat next to him in math. He'd been a reclusive kid even then, *but he seemed nice enough. How could he become a murderer? Could he really have hurt Julie? Maybe somebody should do some poking around. Maybe I should call Kal. Huh, what a waste of time that would be. They never found her killer. As I remember it, they found Zach with her blood on his clothes, and that was it. They didn't bother to look any further. Typical! Jim Burns got her pregnant and married her right out of high school. The family was in an uproar.*

Mallory shook her head, trying to rid her mind of the graphic images it conjured of Wynona Burns' body. *But they never found it, did they? Just a whole lot of blood.*

She turned away from the register, looked around the room, grabbed a bus bin, rounded the end of the bar and bussed the empty tables, checking in on the half dozen patrons along the way.

She dumped the bin out back and returned to the bar.

Oh, dear God, she thought as she stared out across the dimly lit, dismal room. *How I hate this place.*

She sat down on a stool behind the bar and stared up at the stains, and inevitably, her thoughts returned to Julie.

Is she dead? Is she lying out there somewhere injured? Did someone take her? Was it criminals, or witches, or Zach Burns? Oh God, what if she's being held prisoner and...

It didn't bear thinking about. "This is ridiculous," she muttered. "Someone needs to do something. And I know who."

6

TUESDAY EVENING LATE

By the time Tucker arrived back at his office that evening —a purpose-built extension to his home on East Brainerd Road—the clouds had rolled in and it had begun to rain.

He locked the door behind him and tossed the plastic bag containing Mallory Carver's files onto his desk, then stood for a second contemplating them.

"Geez," he muttered. "Really?"

And yet... he thought *it's entirely possible she's done some of my work for me.* While his experiences with amateur sleuths —and there had been several of them—hadn't been stellar, the one big difference with this one was that she *cared*, and she was determined to find her niece, and so was he.

He shook his head, made himself a cup of coffee, then stood once more before the intimidating stack of... what? He had no idea, and so, with a sigh, he sat down and picked up the first of the five folders, the one she'd claimed was the summary. Each of the documents was labeled with different colored inks. Snippets of information she deemed important were highlighted in different colors, denoting how important she considered them to be. And, of course, there was a helpful color key on a sticky note inside the folder, and he used it constantly as he sorted through the documents.

He hadn't been at it long before he realized he'd been wrong about her. The files contained a wealth of information, all in order and properly tabulated.

The summary folder contained a collection of excellent arguments against the sheriff's—and his own—statements that Julie had left of her own volition. There were copies of a number of text conversations with several of Julie's friends that indicated she'd had some very specific plans for the near future; a level of social planning that didn't mesh with the idea of an impulsive, last-minute fling. Even the emoji-laden conversation he'd spotted earlier had a helpful translation guide of sorts, and the actual text indicated that the two girls had planned for the upcoming music festival—Riverbend—for months. There was a credit card statement to back this up, showing the purchase of a 3-day VIP ticket from an online venue for the sum of $350—not something a frugal young woman would willingly toss away.

There were text, email and Facebook records that proved Julie had been in constant contact with friends and family right up to the day she disappeared. All of that stopped, seemingly on a dime, the morning she walked off into the Cherokee National Forest with her dog Tobin. None of it was rocket science. It was all available to a diligent police detective... *So why the hell didn't they do it?* he wondered, staring at the door. *If they had, they couldn't have come to any other conclusion other than something must have happened to her.*

He stared at the file and decided he would need to

interview Julie's friends, but there were notes that hinted Mallory had already done so. Again, he wondered how far and by how much the young lady had jumped his investigation. He smiled at the thought, then set about locating the folder containing the interviews, with colored diagramming added. But he came across the folder with trail maps first.

Now this is some really solid work, he thought as he opened one of the maps.

Mallory had broken the trails down multiple ways: each trail had its own separate map with hand-written notes about the degree of difficulty. Each set of trails that intersected one another had a map, again with hand-written notes, and he was amazed how some trails came within speaking distance of each other, only to have sheer drop-offs or other geographical disadvantages to hikers, or hunters.

How could anyone know all this? Mallory must have walked every trail, many times. She must have an exceptional memory for detail. And the amount of work...

He sat back in his chair, linked his fingers together behind his neck and stared at the FBI vest hanging on the back of the door.

He sat for several minutes contemplating the maps spread across his desk, then leaned forward and picked up the map of the Red Grove trail.

The hiking difficulty of trails is determined by the National Parks Service by a series of scales numbered from 50-200. Anything under 50 is considered easy walking; 50-100 moderate; 100-150 moderately strenuous; 150-200 strenuous and a challenge; greater than 200 extremely strenuous only to be attempted by experienced, well-prepared hikers. Mallory had rated Red Grove 150, strenuous, and one of her and Julie's personal trail preferences. *So, she's a hiker, too. Interesting.*

There was also a note that, according to her sister, Jennifer, it was the trail Julie planned to hike the day she disappeared.

There were also notes that suggested the county sheriff's department had, so far, declined to search the areas. Their reason being that Julie's Bronco had not been found at either of the trailheads—there were two of them serving the eastern and western branches of the trail—and that indicated she'd left the area of her own volition and would no doubt return in due course.

There has to be a better reason than that, he thought and made a note to check in at the sheriff's office in the morning.

According to Carver's research, there's a high incidence of missing person cases in the area, and that makes me wonder if maybe there's a trafficking operation. That would be a whole other kettle of fish. And according to this, the purpose of her hike that day was work-related. She was supposed to be inspecting the trail. Hmm. If that's the case, why the blazes haven't the authorities searched the trail? It makes no sense; no sense at all.

For several hours he continued to work his way through Mallory's file until, at a little after eleven, a loud clap of thunder startled him, disrupting his concentration. He blinked, stood up and realized he was still wearing his Glock.

He slipped off his shoulder holster, walked over to the gun safe, and was just about to close the safe door and return to his desk when there was a frantic knock on the door.

What the hell? he thought as he glanced at his watch. *Who the blazes can that be?* He grabbed the Glock and

CHAPTER 6

stepped carefully to the window overlooking the office front step and peered out.

Standing there in the downpour, her hair plastered to her face, was Mallory Carver.

"Oh, for Pete's sake," he muttered and opened the door. "Well, don't just stand there. Come on in."

She stepped inside, her clothes and hair dripping wet.

"Thank you, thank you, thank you," she mumbled, stripping off her coat and handing it to him. "It's kind of..." she trailed off, looked at him for a second or two, then launched into a rapid-fire jumble of words.

"Okay. So I'm sorry to disturb you this late, but I had to talk to you. You see, I was at work, at The Saloon, and Vinnie—he's my boss—was being kind of a jerk, and I was trying to explain how nobody listens to me, only he wasn't listening to me either—"

"Hold on," Tucker said, interrupting her. "You're soaking wet. Let me get you some towels."

She nodded and continued, "...and I told him he was a jerk because he wasn't listening, but he told me I should just accept the fact that my niece was probably already dead. And then I talked to Howie, and he told me..."

He opened the adjoining door to his house, stepped into the bathroom, grabbed two large bath towels and handed them to her as she continued without a pause.

"... and Howie—he's a customer; comes in every night—told me there are a whole bunch of weirdos living up there around Red Grove, like moonshiners and pot farmers and maybe witches, too, who do crazy things at night. And then he reminded me of a guy who lives up there who everyone thinks killed his mother. He was charged with it, but he was never convicted, and he lives in a shack up on the mountain and hunts with a big bow. And Howie said maybe he killed my niece for some reason, but

I don't know why he would and... and you..." She looked at him and, for the first time since he'd opened the door, she actually seemed to see him.

"And you aren't listening to me either, are you?"

He stepped closer to her, put a hand on each of her shoulders, and said, "Relax. Take it easy, okay?"

She bit her bottom lip, looked into his eyes, and he watched as a tear rolled down each of her cheeks.

"The bathroom's just through that door," he said gently. "Dry yourself off and then come and sit down."

She was gone no more than a few minutes, and when she returned, she stopped halfway across the room, stared at the papers spread across his desk and said, her voice catching, "Are those my files?"

He looked at them, then said, "Yes. I wanted to ask you about the interviews—"

"You read them?" she whispered.

"I... Yes, of course I read them... well, some of them. There's a lot here, and I have a way to go yet."

"You actually read my files," she said in disbelief.

"I read your files. Now, please sit down. You look as if you're about to collapse."

"I'm... I'm sorry, Mr. Randall," she said as she sat down in one of the two wingback chairs in front of his desk, the one so recently occupied by her sister. "Jennifer says nobody can understand me when I do that."

"Do what?" he asked, knowing the best way to get her to focus was to talk her down until she was calm.

"I get emotional and talk a mile a minute. Motormouth is what she calls me. I usually have more control, but Julie is like my sister, and it hurts all the time, and I don't know how to deal with it. She's... dead, isn't she?"

"Never say dead," he replied, then stared at her, not knowing what else to say. He wanted to reach out and take

CHAPTER 6

her hand and tell her everything was going to be all right, but instead, he said, "Can I get you something? Tea? Coffee?"

"Coffee, please," she replied.

He stood and went to the coffee maker.

"How do you—"

"Black please."

He nodded, scooped the beans into the grinder and ran it for a few seconds.

"You take your coffee seriously," she said. "I've never seen anyone grind their own beans before."

"You get a much better flavor that way," he said.

There was another awkward silence, then he said, "Okay. Well, let me grab a new notebook."

"Why do you need a notebook?" she asked.

"Don't you have some new information for me?" he asked.

She blinked as though she'd forgotten. "Oh. Right. Yes. Of course."

He took a notepad from his desk drawer, then went to the coffeemaker, poured some into a mug and handed it to her.

"Careful, it's…" Hot, he was going to say, but before he could finish, she grabbed the mug in both hands and took a sip.

"Oh, wow," she said. "This is so good. What kind of coffee is it? I know it's not the same as the stuff Vinnie serves."

"It's Jamaican," Tucker said. "I order it in. It's expensive, but it's worth it."

"It makes the stuff I usually drink taste like burned water."

"Exactly, which is why…" He paused, hesitated for a moment, then grabbed his notebook and pen, sat down beside her and said, "All right, down to business. So a bear came into The Saloon and told you about some witches? That was about all I was able to grasp from your... tirade." He smiled at her and nodded.

She looked at him over the rim of her mug, her eyes wide.

"Go ahead," he said, "fire away."

"Where d'you want me to begin?"

"At the beginning," he replied.

7

Mallory sipped her coffee and breathed a sigh of relief. *Finally, somebody wants to listen to me.*

It must have been twenty minutes or so later when she finished telling him about her conversation with Howie O'Neal, and by then she'd finished her coffee.

"...and that's about it," she said, looking at him expectantly. "What d'you think?"

He looked up from his notebook, nodded and said, "I think I'd like to know more about this Zach Burns."

"So Jim Burns, Zach's father," she began, "was, I dunno, eighteen? And he was a jerk; came from a wealthy family. He was a star football player, you know, who scored with all the girls. Well, he got one pregnant, Wynona Williams. Nobody knows for sure, but a lot of people think her daddy told him if he didn't make it right, he better not ever find him alone. So Jim married her, and they had a boy, Zach... Look, I only know this from what I've been told. Zach is the same age as me."

Tucker nodded but said nothing.

"So that was good," she continued, "but Jim and

Wynona didn't get along. Then one day, something happened to Jim, and he died. Doc Williams said that he fell and banged his head, but there was a lot of gossip. You know how that goes, right?"

Again, Tucker nodded, so she continued, "Wynona stayed on in the cabin on the mountain until one day she disappeared. They found a whole lot of blood in the cabin, but they didn't find her body or a weapon. What they did find was Zach lying semi-comatose, on the floor, inside the cabin with a huge knot on his head and Wynona's blood on his clothes. He was almost eighteen at the time. He was arrested and charged with Wynona's murder. But the charges were dropped for lack of evidence. After they dropped the charges, he just disappeared one day, and no one cared. Good riddance, most people around here thought. A lot of people said bad things about him, including my dad; he was kinda loud back then."

"And now he's back?" Tucker asked.

"So Howie says."

"And he's living in the cabin on the mountain?"

"Yup. That's what he said."

She fell silent. Tucker finished writing his notes, then he read through them.

"Well—" he began.

"Look, I'm sorry," she blurted. "Everything I said sounds like some kooky conspiracy theory, doesn't it?"

"No, it—"

"It does. It all sounds so stupid, but she's been gone a whole week, and every morning I wake up and grab my phone hoping there'll be a text from her... or even from Jennifer telling me she's okay. That she's been found."

She looked away and wiped at her eyes.

"I just feel like every little detail counts. I don't want to

CHAPTER 7

overlook anything. I want to provide you with the best possible shot at finding her."

He nodded, flipped through the pages of the notebook once more before closing it, then looked at her and said, "As much as I'd like to go through all of this information with you, it's getting late, and we need to get some sleep."

She looked at the clock on the wall. It was almost two in the morning.

"Oh, good Lord," she said and rose to her feet. "I'm so sorry. I didn't think... I didn't mean to keep you up so late."

"Comes with the business," he said. "I was already up when you got here. Besides, I wasn't finished going through your files. I probably wouldn't have called it a night until now, anyway. Um..." He hesitated. "I have a couch, and if you need a shower or something... Well, anyway, you can stay here if you need to." He looked uncomfortable, as if he didn't know what else to say.

"No, it's fine," she said. "I need to go home.

"Of course," he said, "I suppose you have someone waiting for you."

"Oh no, I'm single," she blurted out, then immediately regretted it. *Just sound lonely and desperate, why don't you, Mallory?*

"So you're going to see the police tomorrow morning?" she asked.

"Um..." He hesitated. "Yes, but it will be quite a busy day. After that, I'll be heading up 64 to take a look at the Red Grove trail."

Mallory cocked her head and narrowed her eyes. "Not by yourself, you're not. Red Grove is a seriously tough trail and not for amateurs, especially alone. I'll take you. I know it well. Julie and I hiked it together many times. I'll pack us some trail mix and some water, and I'll bring Annie—she's my dog—so don't worry about bringing anything. The sheriff's department opens at seven. Could we meet up at Hardee's on Shallowford at, say, seven-thirty?"

"Yes, that will work, I guess," he said hesitantly.

Mallory turned back to him. "I'm going to leave talking to the police to you, though, if that's okay. Most of the cops at the sheriff's department don't seem to like me. Can't think why." She shrugged and gifted him with a cheeky grin.

Tucker shook his head. "I can only imagine," he said wryly.

As Mallory drove home that morning, she tried to analyze everything she'd said and every response he'd made. She wanted to believe she'd been helpful but was having a hard time convincing herself.

She lived alone in a small community just outside the city limits, with only her Border Collie, Annie, for company. Home was a modest farmhouse on an acre of sloping land with a distant view of the mountains to the east, and it was some twenty minutes after leaving Tucker's office she pulled into the driveway. She stopped the car in front of the garage door, turned off the motor, set the parking brake, and then sighed and shook her head. She'd lived there for a little more than seven years, ever since her mom had passed away. She'd paid for it with her share of her mother's will and insurance money. She was one of those rare, debt-free individuals, and she was proud of it.

She stepped out of the car—the rain had stopped. The sky had cleared, and the half-moon, still fairly high in the western sky, every now and then dipped behind a fast-scudding cloud. She could hear the hooting call of an owl and the gentle sound of the night breeze passing through the trees. It was a peaceful moment, but she couldn't shake off the feeling that something wasn't quite right. She sighed, stared at the silhouette of the dark and distant mountains on the skyline, then shook her head and turned and walked around the garage to her back door, stepped up onto the deck and took her keys from her pocket.

As she opened the door, Annie ran out, her tail swishing back and forth excitedly.

Mallory bent down, petted the dog, then stepped aside and said, "Go on, girl. I'm sure you need to go. I meant to come straight home after work and let you out, but something came up; you know how it is, right?" Then she stepped inside and flipped on the porch light, feeling more than a little guilty about leaving the dog alone for so long.

"Hey, girl," she said as the dog rushed back inside several moments later. "Maybe I should get you a friend. You'd like that, huh?"

Annie wagged her tail.

"Yeah. That's what we'll do... not a boyfriend, though." She looked sternly at the dog. "Maybe a cute little Jack Russell. What d'you think about that?

The dog panted her approval, then ran to her bowl, turned her head and looked at her.

Mallory nodded and filled her bowl, then sat at the kitchen table and thought for a minute: *A shower,* she decided. *A hot shower is exactly what I need.*

Carefully, she locked the back door, checked the front door and drew the curtains and shades. Only then did she strip down and head upstairs to the bathroom.

The almost scalding water felt wonderful on her chilly skin. She reveled in the warmth until, finally, with the water cooling, she shut it off, stepped out and toweled herself off.

She'd just drawn her robe tight around her and was on

her way to her bedroom when... she heard something downstairs.

What was that? She stood still, listening; nothing. *It's just my imagination... Oh, m'God. There it is again.*

She looked at Annie. The dog was on the alert, her ears pricked. She looked up at her.

"It sounds like there's someone on the back porch, Annie."

Thump! Thump!

Footsteps! Those are definitely footsteps.

She ran downstairs.

"Oh, dear God. Where did I leave my phone?"

She ran to the heap of damp clothes she'd left on the floor of the utility room, fumbled the phone out of the back pocket of her jeans and punched in 9-1-1, and then she paused. The sounds had stopped. Outside, she could hear the wind picking up, the branches of the Japanese maple slapping against the wood siding.

It's just the wind. I must be turning paranoid. She cleared the phone and set it down on the table, then walked into the kitchen.

Thump! Thump! Scrape! Scrape! There it was again, only this time it was accompanied by growling.

Annie barked, bared her teeth and growled.

Oh God, what is it? A bear? She ran to the mantle and grabbed the keys to the gun case, ran to it, unlocked it, grabbed her father's double-barreled shotgun, slid two shells into the chambers and snapped it closed.

Then, listening intently, she crept toward the back door. The growling had stopped. Now all she could hear was something whining, and it sounded familiar. She paused, frowning. She waited. The whining stopped, and then, there was... nothing.

She took a deep breath, unlocked the door and pulled it open.

"Tobin?"

She snapped on the porch light. Julie's dog was lying flat out on the deck, gasping.

"Tobe. Tobe, come here," she whispered and laid the gun down on the floor. The dog crawled toward her. On her knees now, she grabbed him and pulled him into her arms. He whined and licked her face.

"Good boy, Tobe. You came home. You... you came home," she stammered, nuzzling and kissing his cheek. She leaned back and looked at him. He was filthy and thin, much thinner than she'd ever seen him; she could feel his ribs. His fur was matted with what Mallory prayed was mud and not dried blood. "Where's Julie, Tobe?" she muttered. "Where is she?"

8

WEDNESDAY MORNING

Late as it was when he went to bed, sleep didn't come easy. Details of the Romero case kept circling through his mind, and he couldn't shake the nagging feeling that he was missing something, something important.

Barely had he fallen asleep, so it seemed, when he was awakened by his office doorbell. He'd texted Debbie before Mallory had arrived that evening, asking her to come in early. He looked at the bedside clock. It was seven-twenty-five.

"Damn," he muttered as he scrambled out of bed.

With no time to shower, he washed and dressed quickly, ran down the stairs, told Debbie good morning and what needed to be done, and then headed out.

It was almost eight-fifteen when Tucker pulled into the Hardee's parking lot that morning. He was late, something he'd rarely tolerate in others.

It wasn't until he saw his reflection in the restaurant's glass door that he realized he'd forgotten to shave. He hesitated for a moment, considering whether or not to drive to the drugstore to buy an electric razor. But he was already late, and even though he'd not seen Mallory's pickup in the parking lot, she *was* a client, and for him not to be there when she arrived would be unprofessional. So he sighed, pushed through the door and ordered a coffee and a sausage and egg biscuit.

He briefly considered ordering something for Mallory, but not knowing what she'd like to eat, he decided against it. He paid for his order and sat down at a table near the front window, where he had a view of Amnicola Highway and the Chattanooga Police Department.

He watched the early morning commuters making their way into the city. *Where the hell is she?* he wondered, glancing at his watch. It was almost eight-thirty. What little was left of his coffee had gone cold, and his biscuit was long since gone. He took out his phone and checked to see if he had any messages, but then realized they'd not exchanged phone numbers and the only way to get in touch with her was to call her sister, Jennifer, something he didn't want to do.

I guess she overslept, he thought. *She looked like she was running on fumes last night... this morning.*

But he wasn't upset. He'd already gleaned what useful information he could from her files and last night's conversation. And he liked to work alone anyway.

As he sat there, absently staring out the window, watching for her car, he noticed a cherry red Camaro turn into the PD front entrance and park in one of the visitor's spots. He couldn't tell exactly what year the car was, but it appeared to be an 80s model, and even from across the highway he could see it had been fully restored. *Must be worth a tidy sum. I wonder who it belongs to?*

He smiled and nodded as the man he recognized as

CHAPTER 8

Sheriff Cundiff stepped out of the car. *He's way out of his jurisdiction. What's he doing here, I wonder.*

Cundiff, an older man, tall with white hair, a heavy gut and a military bearing, closed the car door, locked it and then walked purposefully into the PD, ignoring the ragtag gathering of people and uniformed officers loitering around outside the building. *Impressive. The man has an imposing presence. I wonder what he's doing here? Only one way to find out,* he thought.

Amnicola at nine-fifteen on a weekday morning can be something of a nightmare, but fortunately, there's a traffic light at the corner of Amnicola and Wisdom.

He waited for the red light, then dashed across Amnicola, then Wisdom, into the PD parking lot and up the front steps, through the doors and into the foyer where the female duty sergeant—who reminded him a bit of Debbie—was smiling down at her computer, which indicated—to him anyway—that she was looking at something other than work.

"Excuse me," he said. "I'd like to speak with Sheriff Cundiff. I saw him come in a few minutes ago."

The sergeant looked up at him, narrowed her eyes, and said, "He's in with Chief Johnston. Does he know you?"

Tucker shook his head. "No, but it's kind of important. Please tell him that it's Tucker Randall and that I'd like to talk to him about the Julie Romero case."

She frowned at him but picked up the phone and, after a short, one-sided conversation, looked at him and said, "If you'll take a seat, sir. Sheriff Cundiff will be with you shortly."

Tucker nodded, stepped away from the desk, sat down near the window and glanced out across the road, briefly wondering if Mallory was awake yet.

He hadn't been seated for more than a few minutes when Sheriff Cundiff appeared in the doorway.

"All right, boy," he said. "You want to see me. Here I am."

Tucker, mildly annoyed that the sheriff addressed him in such a dismissive, diminutive tone, rose to his feet and strode purposefully toward the man, his expression blank.

"It's nice to meet you, Sheriff," Tucker said, offering his hand. "I'm Tucker Randall."

"I know who you are," he snapped, gripping his hand firmly. "What d'you want?"

Tucker, realizing this was going to be a public, stand-up meeting, looked Cundiff in the eye and said, "The Romero family has hired me to find their daughter, Julie. As you already know, she's been missing for more than a week."

"You're here for the Romero girl?" Cundiff raised his eyebrows.

"I am, and I was hoping I could get a look at the file," Tucker said bluntly. "I'm thinking that maybe we could collaborate and find the kid sooner rather than later."

"There is no case file," the sheriff snapped, "and if there was, it would be in my office in Benton. But see, there's no reason to think she's missing. You're wasting your time, son." He glared sternly at Tucker, then continued. "Not to mention wasting police time and the people's hard-earned money. Now see here, you just dragged me out of a meeting with the chief—"

"Then how do you explain Julie's disappearance?" Tucker said, interrupting him.

"Now lookie here, Randall. You know as well as I do that Chattanooga ain't exactly the place young folks want to be anymore, and my boys haven't been able to locate that Bronco of hers, so the consensus is that she just up and left."

"Oh, come on, Sheriff," Tucker replied. "Surely, you're

CHAPTER 8

not buying into that. What about the forest, the trails? Why haven't they been searched?"

"Because there was nothing to indicate she was ever out there," Cundiff replied, a little uneasily. "No car. No-thing!"

"You're wrong, Sheriff," he said, anger slowly building inside him. "I've read her journal, and it puts her right there, on Red Grove trail."

"She's twenty-three, son!" Cundiff replied. "Kids are fickle at that age, and like I said, my boys didn't find her Bronco. It wasn't in the lot at either of the two trailheads. She was never there."

"The fact that you didn't find her car doesn't mean a damn thing, and you know it," Tucker snapped. "How do you know she wasn't kidnapped? Someone could easily have taken her and her car. It's been eight days, for God's sake. Why the hell aren't you out there looking for her?"

As soon as he raised his voice, two uniformed officers stepped up.

"You got a problem here, Sheriff?" one of them asked.

"Boys," Cundiff said with a slight smile on his lips, "I think our friend, Mr. Randall, here, needs some fresh air. Kindly escort him out of the building, would you?"

A strong hand gripped his shoulder. Tucker shrugged it off. "I can take myself out."

He looked Cundiff in the eye and said, "Thank you for taking the time and for the conversation, Sheriff. As enlightening as it was, I think I'll need to speak with the police chief in Benton and then head up there and take a look at the Red Grove trail myself."

The sheriff laughed and shook his head. "I'm telling you, Randall," he said. "The kid just took off. There's no case. And... if you do go poking around up there, good luck to you."

Tucker nodded, turned and walked across the foyer to

the door, opened it, then turned and looked back at the sheriff.

"I'm warning you, Randall. Stay out of the forest. If not, you'd best be careful. There's been plenty of folks who've gone up there and never come back."

Was that a threat? he wondered. *Are you kidding me?*

Tucker cocked his head, smiled at him, and walked out of the building. He'd lived in Tennessee all his life and he knew there were some weird goings on up there in the mountains, but he also knew that most of it was folklore, tall tales, urban legend. He also knew that that kind of garbage didn't make experienced woodsmen go missing. Julie *knew* the forest, and he knew deep in his gut that she was still out there somewhere, and he was more determined than ever to find her.

He was halfway across the street when his phone buzzed. He took it from his pocket and glanced at the screen. It was Jennifer Romero. He accepted the call.

At first, he couldn't understand a word she was saying because she was talking so fast.

"Slow down, Jennifer," Tucker said gently. "Tell me what's wrong?'

"Please," she said. "You have to get over here now."

"What's going on, Jennifer?" Tucker asked, a sinking feeling in his gut. *Oh, geez. Please don't tell me they've found her body.*

"It's… It's… Please. Just come. I'm at Mallory's house. She's found Julie's dog, Tobin."

He froze for a moment until someone honked at him. He was still in the middle of the street.

He strode to his car. "I'm on my way," he said as he started the car. "Give me the address."

9

WEDNESDAY 9:30AM

Mallory was seated at the kitchen island, elbows resting on the quartz surface, face buried in her hands, desperately searching for a hopeful scenario—one where her niece was alive and well and Tobin's appearance wasn't an indication of... what, she didn't know. And, for the first time in her life, she felt sure she had a real connection with her sister.

Jennifer and Jared were huddled together on Mallory's living room floor with Tobin.

Julie would never abandon Tobin, she thought. *Maybe she's hurt? It's possible, right? She could have fallen while out on the trail... broken a bone or twisted her ankle. If she couldn't walk, maybe she sent Tobin to find help? He might be able to lead us right to her.*

Despite the holes in such a scenario, Mallory clung to the hope that Julie would soon be found and all would be well.

But if she's injured, why doesn't she call? Bad service? No; there are cell towers all along the top of the mountain. Maybe her phone died? No. Julie carries two backup chargers, but what if both died? No. That can't happen. Why haven't the forest rangers found her? They travel those trails every day, and Red Grove isn't exactly a secluded spot... What if she slipped and tumbled into a gully and dropped her phone? That's possible, right? But she wouldn't have her phone turned off, would she? So why is it going straight to voice mail and where is her car? How do we know she isn't dead?

Before she could come up with a reasonable answer to that one, however, there was a knock at the door.

She slid off the stool, saying, "I'll get it. It must be Mr. Randall."

If Jennifer heard her, she made no sign. Jared looked up and nodded as she went to the front door and opened it.

"Hey. Sorry I let you down," she said, "but... Well, you'll see. Come on in."

"Your sister called me, and—"

"Yeah, I know," she said as he stepped inside. "They're both here, Jennifer and Jared, but they're in a bit of a state. I'm not sure they'll want to talk to you right now. My sister's hardly said a word since she called you, but, well, we'll see. You want some coffee? It won't be like you make it, but I like it."

Tucker nodded. "Sure. That would be nice. Thank you."

"Good. Follow me. We'll go through to the kitchen."

She was worried he was going to ask her how *she* was doing, something she would have appreciated at any other time, but not then. She was barely holding it together, and she knew if he asked, she'd break down and cry, and that wasn't an option.

But, he didn't. Instead, he merely nodded and said, "Where are they?"

"In the living room; this way."

"Jennifer, Jared," she said. "Mr. Randall's here."

Jennifer looked up at them, her face white, tear-stained, holding Tobin tight against her chest.

"I'm sorry, Mr. Randall," Jared said. "We... that is I... can you give us a moment, please?"

"Of course," Tucker said. "Take as long as you need." Then he looked at Mallory, his eyebrows raised.

"This way," she said and led him into the kitchen.

"Please, sit down. How d'you like your coffee?" she asked.

"Better than what I had this morning, I hope," he replied, smiling, then added, "Black will be fine, thank you."

He took a seat at the kitchen table. She poured two cups, set one down in front of him, then sat down opposite him.

There followed a moment of awkward silence while she waited for him to say something, but he didn't. He just looked around her kitchen.

Finally, unable to bear the silence any longer, she picked up a saltshaker and said, "I found this at a yard sale a couple of years back. I paid ten dollars for it."

He took it from her, smiled and said, "It looks like a baby Elvis that ate a pound of bacon. So go on. Tell me. How much is it really worth?"

She smiled. "That's the thing about antiques. You never really know what you're getting. An Elvis buff would look at it and see a tchotchke. A collector might recognize it as a rarity. It was made in 1956, and it is quite rare. Depending on who's at the auction house, anywhere between fifty and five hundred."

"So," he said. "You're an antiques collector. I didn't expect that."

Not sure if the comment was a jab or a compliment,

Mallory smiled at him and said, "Oh, I'm just full of surprises."

I bet you are, he thought.

He pointed to the centerpiece and said, "And that? Where did you get it?"

"That's a Fenton Art Glass bowl," she replied. "I paid fifty dollars for it two years ago at an estate sale. It's worth more than three hundred."

"Really?" He sounded surprised and not a little impressed.

"Really," she said.

And so it continued for some twenty minutes more until finally Jared poked his head through the door and beckoned them and said, "Jen's feeling a little better, if you'd like to join us."

Jennifer was still sitting on the floor with Tobin beside her, his head resting on her thigh, his eyes closed, twitching restlessly as if he was having a nightmare, while Jennifer slowly, gently stroked his head.

Tucker looked down at the dog, grimaced, then he turned to Mallory and said, "Have you reported this to the police?"

She shook her head. "No, I haven't. I doubt it would do any good. They'll just say Julie dumped him and left the state... or something."

"We'll have to tell them," he said. "We need to organize a search party, and they have the resources; we don't."

Mallory frowned. "What are you smoking?" she asked. "They're not going to do that. The cops are... They won't go into the woods. They're scared... They're scared of the moonshiners and boogie men who're supposed to live up there."

Jared snorted, laughed harshly and said, "In all my years in the business, I've never seen any of that crap." He paused reflectively, then continued, "That being said, I do know there are moonshiners operating up there, and pot and ginseng growers, but they're harmless enough, as long as you don't mess with them or their grow. But Julie knows better than to interfere or get tangled up with them; and most of them know her anyway. They wouldn't harm her. Though I have heard rumors about a trail they're supposed to run all the way up through the Appalachians into Virginia, but it's off the maps and probably just hearsay."

"Hmmm..." Tucker said, almost to himself. "That's interesting."

Mallory could almost hear the gears turning inside his head as he considered it.

But didn't Jared just say that it was all hearsay? she thought. *What could he possibly be thinking that would cause him to frown like that?*

She reached out, touched his arm and said, "Hey, what are you thinking?"

He turned his head, looked at her and said, "I... nothing. It was nothing. Look, as interesting as all this is, right now my concerns are with Tobin." He nodded toward the sleeping dog. "We have to report it to Sheriff Cundiff because, at the end of the day, he's the one who'll organize the search. And we need to take Tobin to the vet, poor thing."

Jared looked upset but didn't argue.

Jennifer nodded firmly in agreement. "They'll have to listen to us now, won't they?" she asked. "Hopefully, it isn't..."

She didn't finish, but Mallory knew what she was thinking. *Hopefully, she's wrong.*

"Good," Tucker said. "So, now that's decided, I have a couple of questions. Are you up to it?"

Jennifer and Jared nodded.

"Of course," Mallory said. "Whatever you say. We'll do everything we can to help."

"Geographically speaking," Tucker said, looking at Jared, "is there any reason why Tobin came here instead of going home?"

"I don't know why he would. It's not much closer," Jared replied. "Not in terms of distance, anyway."

Mallory nodded. "He's smart. He wouldn't have gone into the city because he'd be afraid of the traffic. I don't know how he could have made it all the way here. It must be forty miles, or more, from the Red Grove trailhead to here."

"You're sure that's where she went?" Tucker said.

"That was the plan," Jared replied. "She was going to inspect the trail. We have outings planned from now through the end of September."

"Julie and I take the dogs up there all the time and let them run off-leash," Mallory said. "Tobin knows the trails and the area about as well as Annie does."

"Annie?" Tucker asked.

"Oh. Yes," Mallory said, realizing she hadn't introduced her yet. "She's my dog. I put her in my room because she kept worrying Tobin and whining. I can bring her out to meet you… if you like."

But Tucker was already thinking ahead. "I want to take a look at that trail myself, but first, we must notify the police."

Jared frowned. "I wish I could help. But between the limp and the arthritis… Well, I'd just slow you down."

Mallory could see tears glistening in his eyes. Jennifer grasped his hand and squeezed it. Mallory swallowed hard, wanting to say something comforting, but she feared she would only make matters worse if she tried.

"I'll take you," she said. "I know those trails almost as well as Julie. We'll take Annie with us."

Tucker nodded.

"We really do need to get Tobin to the vet," Jennifer said. "We'll call Sheriff Cundiff. That way, you two can get started. You won't want to waste any daylight."

"Good," Tucker said. "We'll call you if we find anything, so don't worry."

Mallory helped Jennifer load Tobin into a crate and then waved as they backed down the short driveway. She watched as they turned onto the highway, and then, already feeling a little better, she returned to the living room.

"You ready?" she asked. "It's already after eleven. We need to go. My stuff's already in my car. You can leave yours here."

10

WEDNESDAY 11:45AM

The sun was shining brightly, the birds were singing in the treetops and golden beams of sunlight bounced off the moist pine needles that blanketed the forest floor. Verdant green foliage decorated both sides of the Red Grove trail, while a handful of butterflies drifted by on gossamer wings. It was indeed a beautiful day to be out in the forest, but Tucker saw little of that. All he could think about, given Tobin's condition, was what they *might* find.

Having seen the dog, he had no doubt that the poor girl had never left the forest. *Not willingly, anyway*, he thought, breathing hard.

The trail was indeed difficult, and he was finding it hard going.

Mallory, however, was a hiking machine. Her breathing never changed as she strode onward and upward as Annie, her Border Collie, trotted along beside her, dodging this way and that, sometimes running off into the trees only to return to her side a moment later.

Any thoughts he might have had about Mallory's fitness for the task were dispelled, and it was clear she was every bit the trail guide Julie was. *So why doesn't she pursue it?* he wondered.

Unable to think of a reason, he turned his attention back to the trail, looking for anything that appeared to be out of the ordinary, anything that might offer a clue as to what had happened to the missing girl. But by then, he'd already come to the conclusion that she was probably dead.

Never say dead, Tucker, he thought. *Never say dead.*

Mallory's mood, he noted, had greatly improved, but he was worried she might have caught on to what he was thinking. For some reason that he couldn't fathom, however, she seemed almost alarmingly optimistic, and he silently prayed he hadn't raised her hopes, especially when his gut was telling him things would only get darker from here on in.

Tobin looked like he'd been out here alone for the full eight days, he thought. *And if we do find Julie—and it's a big if—I doubt she survived. And even if she did, if she had an accident, a fall, she'd have been easy prey for the wild animals.*

He shook his head and tried to rid himself of the thought, but it lingered and morphed into a scenario he didn't want to contemplate.

Damn it! he thought as he stumbled over a gnarled tree root. *This was a terrible idea. What the hell was I thinking? What will it do to Mallory if we do find Julie? What if she's... Geez, it doesn't bear thinking about.*

For a moment, he considered sending her home, but he could tell from the pep in her step and the way she kept chattering that it would be useless to even suggest it. *There's no way she'll listen to me... no matter what I say.*

CHAPTER 10

He sighed and marched onward, struggling to keep up with her as she strode confidently ahead, still talking. By then, she was some twenty yards ahead of him and he couldn't hear much of what she was saying. Something about Julie and a blackberry bush? And soon he became lost again in a world of his own, thinking about the case, Sheriff Cundiff, and why they hadn't organized a thorough search of the forest and the trails, especially the Red Grove trail. And his gut was telling him that something just wasn't adding up.

His mind was awhirl with dozens of disconnected images: Tobin's muddy fur. Julie's messages about the Riverbend festival. Sheriff Cundiff's expensive car. A rumored trail run by moonshiners. There were so many odd details about the case and, try as he might, Tucker couldn't piece them together in a way that made any sense. Something was missing, but what? The answers were there. He was sure of it. *All I need is the trigger...* he thought as he struggled on over the rough terrain.

A few minutes later, Annie appeared seemingly out of nowhere and slowed to lope alongside him, looking up at him with watery, dark brown eyes.

"Hey, girl," he said and reached down and gently scratched behind her ears while Mallory, now some dozen yards or so ahead, slowed and waited for him to catch up a little, then continued on again, saying something about him trying to keep up. But by then, she'd opened the gap between them again, and Tucker, too busy trying to stay on his feet, heard little of what she was saying.

When he'd first suggested they check out the trail, he'd assumed it would be a well-defined path, like the hiking trails he was accustomed to in and around Chattanooga, well-traveled and easily navigated, but this "trail"... Well, it was hardly that. It was undulating, narrow at times with room for only one person at a time, sometimes densely overgrown, often dark, and everywhere littered with trip and fall hazards. But worst of all were the insects and, for at least the tenth time, he wished he had brought some bug spray with him. *The last thing I need is to contract Lyme disease.*

As he walked, he couldn't help but think about the case he'd turned down in Nebraska and imagined what it might have been like had he made the more intelligent decision. *Smart Tucker,* he thought, *would still be in the preliminary stages of a challenging but interesting murder investigation. Smart Tucker wouldn't have to worry about black widow spiders, brown recluses, ticks, two-hundred-pound wild boar, or four-hundred-pound black bears on the hunt for an easy mark like Stupid Tucker. But no. Here I am, knee-deep in bug-infested grass looking for... something useful.*

But it had rained the day before, and he had serious doubts they were going to find anything. Any tracks there might have been would certainly be long gone. *Maybe she dropped something. Maybe her abductor dropped something.* He stopped walking and looked around, taking in the terrain, the dense undergrowth, the trees. *Even if they did, I doubt we'd be able to spot anything in this—*

"Yo, city boy!" Mallory called to him, snapping him out of his thoughts.

She'd stopped, turned around, and was staring back down the trail at him. "Never been hiking before?"

Tucker frowned. "Of course I've been hiking before. On actual trails, not this... this wilderness."

Mallory laughed, a light tinkling sound that echoed through the spring air as gentle and pervasive as windchimes. "So, by that, I assume you mean you've been to the Greenway?"

CHAPTER 10

"Keep smiling," Tucker said as he stopped walking and leaned forward, his head down, hands on his knees.

He lifted his head and looked at her. "This is not your average hiking trail. It's tough, and it's damn dangerous. One wrong step, and you could end up in a copperhead nest."

Mallory rolled her eyes and, laughing, walked easily back down the trail to join him. He straightened up and watched her approach, as sure-footed as a mountain goat.

She stood before him, feet apart, one hand on her hip, the other on the strap of her backpack, and said, "It's not so bad, Mr. Randall. Not if you're used to it, which you're obviously not. I told you, Julie and me, we bring Annie and Tobin up here all the time. I've hiked this trail... I was going to say a hundred times, but that wouldn't be true. It's like... forty or fifty, I guess. Anyway, if their scent isn't enough to keep the snakes away, then you can bet that Annie would at least bark and let us know if there was anything dangerous nearby. She's such a good girl." She bent down and petted her dog affectionately. "Isn't that right, baby?"

Tucker rolled his eyes and said, "At least someone's looking out for me. And please, call me Tucker. Mr. Randall's so... formal."

He bent down to pet Annie; she licked his hand.

"Okay. Tucker it is," she said. "You know, she really likes you. She doesn't usually take to strangers. She's very protective of me. She didn't like *me* that much when I first adopted her."

"Maybe it's the beef jerky I hid in my pocket," he said with a laugh.

"Oh, you have some? Gimme," she demanded, holding out her hand.

"I was kidding," he said, smiling.

He stared up into the canopy. The sun was still high. He looked at his watch—almost ten after one.

"How much further?" he asked. "We've been up here almost two hours, and I don't want to be caught out here at night."

Again, Mallory smiled at him. "Oh come on, softy. Don't tell me the cops have rubbed off on you. Surely, you're not afraid of spending a relaxing night under the stars with little old me?"

He almost choked. "Are you serious? Unless I'm mistaken, there's a cold front moving in, and the lows for tonight are supposed to be in the upper forties. We're not exactly prepared to brave the weather, now are we? And about those stars; have you looked up there? God only knows what's creeping about up there in the treetops."

She looked up, then back at him and said, "Maybe you're right. Come on. We've a way to go yet," and she turned and started back up the trail.

"So how much farther?" he asked again.

She stopped, turned around and looked at him.

"Hmmm... Well, we're almost halfway there now. It's nearly six miles from the trailhead that Julie should've been on that morning. So... a little more than three miles?"

Tucker tried not to think about what three more miles through the forest would be like, desperately hoping that this narrow "trail" would feed into a larger, more traveled path. "Does anyone else hike up this way? Any of the neighbors, perhaps?"

Mallory shook her head as she once again took the lead. "Not really. Most of the people who live out this way are older. They know the trail, but it's been a while since I've seen anyone else on it."

"The farther out you go, though," she continued, "the more likely you are to encounter people. The Clearwater subdivision is a couple of miles or so to the east. It's not very big, but I've seen a few of those kids out here in the woods, but they don't usually stray too far from their homes. The only trouble we've ever had out of them was when an older boy was caught trying to set off firecrackers during the dry season. It could have been disastrous if he hadn't been caught. Forest fires can be devastating, you know."

"Yes, I know," he said dryly, and realizing that Mallory was starting to ramble again, he began once again to pay less attention to her words and more to their surroundings.

"What d'you think happened to Julie?" Mallory asked quietly.

"She could have had an accident," he replied carefully. "She could have fallen…"

"Yeah," Mallory snapped, "or she could have been abducted. Or…"

Or met an unfortunate fate at the claws of a hungry animal? Tucker thought. It was all possible, but his gut was telling him it was unlikely. Julie was an experienced hiker, a hunting guide, and there was something about how Tobin had trekked through the woods, smart enough to make it to Mallory's house, that made Tucker sure the dog would have tried to protect Julie from an animal attack, no matter how big said animal might be. And, as far as Tucker could tell, the dog didn't have a scratch on him.

And then there's always the possibility that Julie disappeared of her own volition. She loved nature and, God forbid, if she'd decided to end her life, wouldn't she do it in a place she felt connected to? It was a remote possibility; Julie didn't seem the type to take her own life, and Tucker knew better than to suggest it to Mallory. And besides, he was confident the girl wouldn't have abandoned her dog. So with accident and suicide out of the picture, what did that leave?

Foul play.

Tucker might not yet know how the pieces of the puzzle fit together, but whatever had happened to Julie, he was now certain a third party was involved... "Argh!"

Had he been watching his footing, he might have seen the rusty barbed wire, but he wasn't, and he didn't. He tripped and hit the ground hard, his left side taking the brunt of the impact.

"Tucker!" Mallory yelled. "Are you okay?"

Before he could assess the damage, she was already beside him, hauling him to his feet; her strength amazed him.

"I'm fine," Tucker replied automatically.

"No, you're not. You're bleeding," Mallory cried, pulling his arm towards her. "Oh, my God. It's really deep! You're going to need stitches."

"What the hell is barbed wire doing way out here?" he said.

"Old-timey moonshiners, probably," Mallory said. "They used it to protect their stills from intruders, but that was a long time ago. They don't do that anymore."

"I know just what to do," she continued as she dropped her backpack, opened it, and took out a small first aid kit and a pocketknife.

"Wait... you're going to stitch me? Out here in the woods?" Tucker blurted.

"No, silly. Of course not," she said. "I'll bandage it up and then we'll go see the doctor." She pulled her shirt tail out of her shorts and tore a strip off the hem.

"It's just a scratch, Mallory," he said, "and I'd rather go to the ER."

CHAPTER 10

"Uh-uh!" she shook her head. "The ER will take forever. I know a good doctor. Just let me help you, okay?"

Against his better judgment, Tucker agreed.

"Good. Now you hold still a minute." And she took a piece of gauze from the kit and neatly bandaged his arm.

"There you go," she said, taking a step back. "We'll have you good as new in no time at all, but first we have to get back down off this mountain."

11

WEDNESDAY 4 PM

It was almost four o'clock when they exited the trailhead onto Highway 64. The drive back to Mallory's house took another thirty minutes, and by the time they arrived, it was already four-thirty.

Mallory let Annie into the house, made sure she had fresh water and something to eat, then ran back out to the car, jumped in, started the motor, put it into reverse and hurtled out onto the highway.

"Look," Tucker said, hanging onto the strap with his right hand, "I think you should take me to the ER—"

"Nonsense," she snapped, interrupting him. "The ER will be packed solid. It always is. Where I'm taking you is closer and you won't have to wait forever."

He shook his head and closed his eyes, not arguing further. "Okay... If you say so, but don't we have to have an appointment?"

"No. It's a walk-in clinic," she said as she rounded a bend, tires squealing.

The first part of the journey passed for the most part in silence as Mallory focused her attention on the road, glancing only now and then at Tucker to see how he was doing. It wasn't good. She could see the bandage was soaked through with blood.

"What's that buzzing?" she asked as they stopped at a red light.

"It's my phone," he replied, taking it gingerly from his pocket. "It's my brother, Nate. I swear he's got supernatural instincts," he said as he declined the call.

"Shouldn't you have answered?" she asked as the light turned green.

Tucker shook his head. "He likes to talk, and if I tell him I'm on my way to get stitches because I had an accident in the woods, he'll pitch a fit, so no, I don't want to talk to him right now."

Mallory chuckled. "You know, I think your brother would get along well with Jennifer. I'm sure she's OCD. Is Nate older than you?"

"By a year," he replied.

"Oh wow. You guys must be close, then. That must have been so cool, growing up together. Is he your only sibling?"

Tucker nodded. "Yes. Thankfully. I don't know if I could have handled more than one Nate."

"Is he a detective, too?" she asked.

"No, but he is a cop, a lieutenant," he replied. "He graduated top of his class at the academy and could have done well, but he just wanted to be a regular state trooper."

He fell silent for a moment. "By the way, I spoke to Sheriff Cundiff this morning. It didn't go well. I'll tell you about it later when this mess is cleaned up," he said, looking at his bandaged arm.

She nodded. "So, how about you? How come you're a PI?"

"I haven't always been a PI," he replied. "I was with the FBI, but that didn't work out so well, so here I am."

"The FBI?" she said, glancing at him. "I'm impressed. What happened?"

"That's... not something I want to talk about," he said, staring straight ahead. He was quiet for a moment, then asked, "So, where exactly are you taking me?"

"I'm taking you to Dr. Wilson," she replied. "He runs a small private practice. Maybe you've heard of him? Everyone around here knows him. He and his wife are very much involved in the local community."

Randall shook his head. "Chattanooga's a big city."

"I guess." She sighed.

She drove on in silence. *Yes,* she thought. *I suppose it is a big city by Tennessee standards, anyway.*

Chattanooga, population one hundred eighty-two thousand, and that many more in Hamilton County, was the fourth largest city in the state. Mallory had lived there all her life, and she knew it inside and out, but she could count on the fingers of one hand how many times she'd traveled further than Nashville or Atlanta. And she often wondered what it would be like to wake up in the morning and look out upon a new horizon.

"Do you have family here?" she asked, breaking the silence.

"Nope. My parents moved to Florida when they retired," he replied. "They live in Panama City. Nate moved to Tulsa. His wife's family lives there."

"And... There's no one else?"

"Not really. Just a few cousins here and there."

"You have a lot of friends, though, right?"

"Really?" he asked, looking at her. "You're beginning to sound like Nate. Yes, I have friends. Not a lot. But quality over quantity, right?"

"I'm sorry," she said. "I didn't mean to pry. So, this is it," she said as she pulled into the parking lot. "It's a small practice, but Doctor Wilson is well-respected and *very* good at his job."

"Hah! I hope you're right," Tucker said, "since I'm about to let him sew me up,"

"You'll be fine," she said as she turned off the engine. "Come on."

And, reluctantly, he followed her into the small white building.

"You're sure about this?" he whispered.

"Oh, don't be such a baby," she replied.

"I'm not," he said, frowning.

A few minutes later, a nurse appeared in one of the doorways and took them through to one of the patient rooms, where they waited in silence until finally, the door opened and the doctor and his nurse stepped inside.

"Hello, Mallory," he said. "What can we do for you today?"

"Nothing for me, Doctor. It's my… friend here. He fell and cut his arm."

Wilson frowned, looking down over the top of his glasses at Tucker's blood-soaked bandage. "So I see," he said.

"I tripped and fell on some rusty barbed wire," Tucker said.

"Well, let's take a look at it," he said as he snapped on a pair of purple latex gloves. "Hold up your arm… Good. Hold it right there."

He glanced at Mallory as he started removing the bloody bandage. "So, what were you two doing that caused this?"

"We were looking for my niece, in the forest," Mallory

said. "She's been missing for more than a week. Mr. Randall is a private investigator."

"Is he now?" Wilson said. "How interesting. And where exactly were you looking?"

"Red Grove," Mallory replied. "D'you know it?"

He shook his head and said to Tucker, "No, but I'd stay out of those woods if I were you. There's no telling what or who you might run into." Then he glanced at Mallory and said, "As a child, this one was in and out of my office with all sorts of little injuries—jumping out of trees, falling off her bike, fighting with the boys. She was a rare one."

"I've matured," Mallory said, embarrassed.

The doctor rolled his eyes and smiled, "That you have, my dear."

"Don't you live up that way somewhere?" she asked.

"No, but I do have a small vacation cabin just outside Archville, on Kimsey Mountain Road," he said as he gently finished removing the blood-soaked gauze. "Hmm. This is deep. I'll have to stitch it. You'll also need an antibiotic."

"I know Kimsey," she said. "It goes all the way up to Highway 68, north of Ducktown."

Wilson didn't answer. Instead, he turned to his nurse and said, "If you'll take him back and prep him for me, please, Mandy. Thank you. In the meantime, Mallory, you can come with me."

Mallory followed him back to the window in the reception area.

"Linda," Wilson said to the receptionist. "If you would, please give Miss Carver the paperwork. I'll be in my surgery with Mr. Randall."

"Of course, Doctor," Linda replied as he walked away. She smiled at Mallory and handed her a sheaf of papers on a clipboard. "There you are, dear. Let me know if you have any questions."

Mallory stared at the top sheet and said, "I'm sorry. I can't answer any of these questions."

"Oh... I thought—"

"He's just a friend," Mallory said.

"Of course. I'm sorry," Linda said, smiling. "Well, never mind. You can help him fill them out when Dr. Wilson's finished with him."

"Thanks," Mallory said, then turned away from the window, sat down and picked up a magazine.

Why would Dr. Wilson embarrass me like that in front of Tucker? she wondered.

Mallory was still absently flipping through an old copy of *Vogue* when, some twenty minutes later, the doctor returned with Tucker, who was several shades paler and clearly in pain.

She stood and took several steps forward. "Would you like me to help you fill this out?" Mallory asked, holding up the clipboard. "I can write for you... if you like."

"Oh no," Dr. Wilson interrupted. "That won't be necessary. Take them home. You can bring them with you when you come back next week. But get this prescription filled *today*, and make sure you take them all. That's a nasty gash you have there, and if it goes septic... well, we won't talk about that. Now, Linda will take your payment. Your credit card will be fine. Good day to you both, what's left of it."

"Thanks for your help, Doctor," Mallory said. "We appreciate it."

Then she turned to Tucker and said, "Come on. I'll take you back to your car... I have a pizza in the freezer. You want to share?"

He looked at her, hesitated, then smiled and said, "Sure. Why not?"

12

WEDNESDAY 7:45PM

Tucker was in a rare mood as he drove back to his office early that evening. His arm was stiff and aching like the devil. He was annoyed with himself for letting Mallory drive him to the doctor's office. He'd enjoyed their conversation, but he knew he'd been over-friendly. He also knew he shouldn't have gone to a private physician—not when working on an assignment that could potentially turn high profile.

Nor did he miss the inference that Dr. Wilson wasn't too impressed with Mallory. At first, he thought he was just kidding around with her, but by the end of the visit, he was sure the doctor was actually a little annoyed with her.

Had she really been that much of a handful in her youth, or was he just annoyed that she'd taken him there instead of the ER?

The drive back to her house where he'd left his car had been... to say the least, entertaining. The pizza was good for store-bought, and so was the cabernet. And, though he was reluctant to admit it, so was the company.

It was almost seven-forty-five when he arrived at his office to find that Debbie had left him a note asking him to call Jennifer Romero.

Bracing himself for the worst, he picked up the phone and made the call.

"Mr. Randall, great news," she said. "I thought you ought to know; they're *finally* going to organize a search."

"That *is* good news," Tucker replied. "So when—"

"Mr. Randall. This is Sheriff Cundiff. We're on speaker. You're more than welcome to join us, but you should know the case is now officially under the jurisdiction of my department, and I expect you to be forthcoming about any information you've gathered so far."

"As long as you promise to do the same," Tucker replied.

He heard the sheriff click his tongue, then say, "Of course. All we want is to find Julie. I have my son, Deputy Kal, here with me. He just came back from the vet's office. Apparently, the dog's not in bad shape so... Hold on a minute, Mr. Randall." He heard him say something to Jennifer, and then he said, "Hold on. I'm going outside."

There was a brief interlude, then Cundiff said, "Okay, it's just you and me now. I have her phone, but they can't hear. I've asked the Romeros not to join the search party. I'm sure I don't have to explain why."

"Of course," Tucker replied, nodding to himself. It was clear the sheriff had the same gut feeling as he did.

"You think she's dead," he said.

"I wouldn't go that far, not yet," Cundiff replied. "There's still a chance she's taken off, but... Well, time will tell. In the meantime, I was wondering if you could talk to

CHAPTER 12

them. I know they want to be at the front of the search, but... Well, I would appreciate it."

"Of course," Tucker replied. "I totally understand. I'll talk to them and Mallory. Anything else?"

"Not that I can think of. Well, only that I'm going to have Kal text Mallory to let her know what's happening, but if you could handle her and the rest of the family for me, we'll be good."

"Of course," Tucker said. "I take it you'll get back to me with the details?"

"Tomorrow morning," Cundiff said. "Six o'clock at the ranger cabin on sixty-four. You know where that is?"

"I can find it," Tucker replied.

"Good. Come prepared for a long day. See you tomorrow, Randall." And with that, he hung up.

So, he thought, *I have to convince the Romeros. That's not going to be an easy conversation. And Mallory? That's going to be impossible.*

13

THURSDAY 6AM

Tucker hadn't been gone more than thirty minutes when Mallory's phone rang.

Jared? she thought. *He never calls me...* She flipped the screen and took the call.

"Jared. What—"

"Mal, where are you?" he asked. "I called your work, but Vinnie said you'd called in. Are you all right?"

"Yes, I'm fine. I'm at home. Is something wrong?"

"No. It's all good. They're organizing a search party. They want to start at first light. There are a lot of volunteers. They're going to search all the trails. We'll work the Red Grove. You up for it?"

"Oh, that's wonderful," she replied. "Of course I'm up for it. Where do we meet and what time do I need to be there?"

"At the ranger cabin on sixty-four at six," he said. "They're rounding up volunteers now. Sheriff Cundiff says they're going to search every trail within ten miles of Red Grove. How did you and Randall do today?"

"We hiked the eastern branch of Red Grove, just partway, though, but we found nothing. Tucker fell and cut his arm and... Oh, never mind. I'll tell you about it later. Is Jen there. Can I talk to her?"

"She's talking to the sheriff," Jared replied. "How is he? Is it bad?"

"Bad enough," she replied. "I had to take him to Doctor Wilson for stitches. He just left—"

"Hey," Jared said, interrupting her. "It looks like Jen has wrapped things up with the sheriff and I need to talk to her. See you in the morning, then?"

"I'll be there!" she replied and hung up.

Finally, she thought. *Something's going to go right! I can feel it.*

It was fifteen minutes to six when Mallory drove into the parking area at the ranger cabin the following morning. The cabin, set back off the road in a small clearing, was some seventy yards east of the western branch of the Red Grove trailhead, which pleased her; the going would be easier than the branch they'd hiked the day before, though not much.

She parked her car in front of the cabin, put Annie on her leash, stepped out and looked around. The only indication of life was a green pickup belonging to one of the forest rangers, the open cabin door, and the overpowering smell of...

Coffee! she thought and went up the steps and into the cabin.

CHAPTER 13

"Hey, Bert, Matt," she said to the two rangers. "What's up?"

She knew them both from hiking in the forest and from The Saloon, where they were both regulars.

"I smell coffee," she said. "Any chance I could have some, please?"

"Sure can," Matt replied. "In the kitchen, he'p yourself. You're here for the search, Mal?"

"Yup!" she replied as she walked through to the kitchen. She grabbed a mug from the sink, washed it out, then filled it with some of the strongest coffee she'd ever tasted.

"You want some?" she yelled.

But before the two rangers could answer, she heard the sound of multiple vehicles entering the clearing.

Coffee in hand, she joined Bert and Matt at the door and watched as another forest green pickup truck pulled up in front of the cabin.

"That's Captain Sweet," Bert said from his desk. "Time to look busy."

Captain David Sweet, the head ranger for the district, climbed out of the truck and said, "Hi, Mallory. It's been a while. Nice to see you again."

"It has," Mallory replied. She and Dave had dated for a while in high school. After they broke up, he dated and then married her friend Sandra Fisher. "How's Sandra?"

He scratched the back of his head. "She's fine, I guess."

Uh, oh, she thought. *That doesn't sound good.*

"I hope all this..." He waved a hand in the direction of the gathering crowd, which now included three sheriff's cruisers and more than a dozen assorted private vehicles. "...works out for you."

He looked at the mug in her hand. "I could use some of that. You want to do the honors while I get this lot sorted?"

"Of course," she replied. "Black?"

"As your hat," he said as he walked away.

Annie pushed up against her leg, tail wagging. Mallory wasn't sure if the dog was just nervous or excited at the prospect of chasing squirrels. "Good girl," she said absently as she reached down and scratched behind her ears. "I don't see Tucker yet, do you?"

It was at that moment her phone rang. She took it from her pocket and glanced at the screen. It was her sister, Jennifer.

"Hi, Jen," she said. "What's up? You're on the way, then? Good. How long will you be? I'm sorry. What did you say? He said what? Are you kidding me? And you agreed? No. That's not going to happen. Leave it with me. See you in a few minutes then."

We'll see about that, she thought with a huff.

By six-fifteen, the lot was full. The numbers had grown to more than seventy-five, by Mallory's count, and included five mounted rangers and four K-9 sheriff's deputies, and by six-forty-five, they were ready to disperse to the various trailheads.

"All right, everybody," Sweet shouted.

"Wait—" she tried to interrupt him, but Deputy Kal Cundiff grabbed her arm.

"Now, Mal," he said, "there's no need for you to be bothering the captain. He's just setting everyone up."

"Yes, I know," she said, jerking her arm away. "I talked to Jen just a few minutes ago, and they want me to stay back with her and Jared. That's not going to happen. We need to be up front."

"No way," Kal said. "We can't have her or you up front. What happens if we find their little girl up there dead? She ain't going to look pretty after all this time, now is she? Not after more than a week."

CHAPTER 13

"Wow, you really are something else, Kal," she snapped. "Maybe if your dad had listened to us and organized it a week ago, we could have been spared all of this. Well, it might be okay with them to stay at the rear, but not me. I'll be with the Red Grove West party, and I'll be at the front because neither your dad, you, nor any of his deputies know the trail better than me. And short of arresting me, there's nothing you can do about it."

"Well, I guess, but Dad—I mean the sheriff—ain't gonna like it."

"Then he can bite me," Mallory snapped and then turned away and marched off to find Sheriff Cundiff and tell him exactly what she planned to do.

She found him on the far side of the clearing, talking to Tucker Randall.

Oh, so he's here? That's good.

"Good morning, Sheriff," she said. "I know my sister has already thanked you, but I'd like to do so, too." She looked around and continued, "This is amazing. There must be almost a hundred people here. Thank you, Sheriff."

Cundiff made a dismissive gesture with his hand. "You don't need to thank me, Mallory. I barely lifted a finger. The county really came through for us, didn't they?"

"They did, but thanks anyway," Mallory said. "Are you going to be leading the search, Sheriff?" She glanced at Tucker. He was looking at his phone.

Cundiff shook his head. "No, I'll be somewhere towards the middle of the Red Grove West group handling communications... Looks like we're about ready to go." He started to turn away.

"Just a minute, please, Sheriff," she said. "I want you to know that I'll be taking a lead position on Red Grove West today. I know that trail better than anyone, and I'll be taking my dog, Annie, with me."

Cundiff stared at her for a moment, his lips clamped together, then he turned to Tucker and said, "I thought you said you were going to deal with this, Randall?" Cundiff snapped.

"I'm sorry, Sheriff, but I think she's right. She does know the trails, and so does her dog. I think they should be out front."

Cundiff frowned, removed his cap, ran his fingers through his thinning red hair, turned to Mallory and said, "No, ma'am. It ain't happening. The best thing you can do right now is stay back and support your sister. She needs you."

"With all due respect, sir," Mallory snapped, "my sister doesn't need anyone, and I'm sure Jared can provide all the support she needs... I need to be up front. And that's where I'm going to be."

After a long moment, the sheriff sighed, scratched his head, replaced his cap, and caved. "Well, I suppose I can't stop you. But you do understand why I want you at the rear with your sister?" He trailed off, giving Mallory a meaningful look.

Her first instinct was to look away, but she managed to hold his gaze. "I do. You think she's dead, don't you, Sheriff?"

"I didn't say that," he snapped. "Aw, hell. Just... do what you want. I can't stop you. Geez, you're one stubborn..." He paused, shook his head and said, "Sheeit!" He turned on his heel and headed toward the rangers.

It was on the tip of her tongue to ask him who'd told him she was stubborn, but she didn't because she already knew the answer, and it was walking toward her, mug in hand, a happy smile on its face.

CHAPTER 13

"Hey, Mal. You talked to my... the sheriff?"

"Yes, Kal. I did," she said resignedly, glancing at Tucker. He looked up from his phone and smiled.

"What did he say?" Kal asked.

"He said we need to get moving."

Sheriff Cundiff walked back to their little group and said, "Kal, you know what to do. Mal... Geez, you go with Kal and do as he says and don't get in the way. You understand?"

It was all she could do to refrain from giving him a smart answer, but instead she said, "Yes, sir."

"Tucker, you can join me whenever you're ready."

Tucker nodded. "Thank you, Sheriff, but I think I'll go with Deputy Cundiff and Mallory."

"Suit yourself," Cundiff said. "Kal, you keep a sharp eye on them, you hear?"

Kal nodded at his father, closed in on Mallory, and suddenly he was standing just a little too close and she took a step back, her hands in the air. "Hey. He said to keep an eye on me, Kal, not smother me. Just keep your distance, okay?"

"I thought you were going to go with the sheriff?" Kal said to Tucker, frowning.

"I changed my mind," Tucker said, smiling at him.

"Yeah, well, okay then," Kal said and turned to face his group of twenty-four people. "Okay, everybody, listen up," he shouted. "We're going to search the western branch of the Red Grove. I'm going to take the lead and stick to the trail. I want you guys to split into two groups of twelve. The first group will take the lead with me and will spread out six on either side of the trail. Try to stay about six to ten feet apart. The second group will follow the first group twenty yards or so behind and do the same. The sheriff and his party will follow on behind. Any questions?"

There were none.

"Now I know it's going to be rough going," he continued, "but we need to do this right, okay? We're looking for anything out of the ordinary. You find anything, anything at all, you stop, stand still, raise your hand and shout, 'Here.' You do *not* touch anything. You got me?"

There was a chorus of yesses.

"All righty, then. Let's go." He looked at Mallory, then at Tucker. "You two are with me then. Follow me and stay close. Understood?"

Mallory gifted him with a withering look. Tucker grinned at her and winked.

"Hey," he whispered as Kal stepped off toward the trailhead. "I enjoyed the pizza last night."

"Me, too," she said. "It was fun. How's the arm?"

"I really don't know," he said. "It hurts a bit, but that's to be expected, I suppose."

"It will be fine," she said, not really knowing what else to say. "Doctor Wilson's a good…"

"Doctor?" he completed the sentence for her, smiling.

"Yes, that," she said. "I'm glad you're here, Tucker. Thank you."

He glanced at her. She was striding along, head down, her eyes on the trail, Annie at her side.

She looked up at him and said, "Hey, eyes on the ground. Watch where you're walking. We don't want a repetition of what happened yesterday."

By then they were some several hundred yards into the trees, and the group had fanned out on each side where the going over the inches-deep carpet of pine needles and rotting leaves was soft, not exactly tough, but it was slow. And Mallory, as experienced as she was, was glad Kal had insisted that she and Tucker stick to the trail.

The deeper into the forest they went, the deeper the

shadows became and the lower the temperature dropped, and Mallory suddenly had an attack of the shivers. She'd known what being at the front meant, and while she thought she was ready to face anything, she knew she could never be fully prepared for...

Oh, heavens, she prayed. *Please don't let us find her dead.*

14

THURSDAY 6:45AM – 8:30PM

Tucker began the search with energy and drive, and for the first hour, he marched steadily onward, his eyes on the ground. Fortunately, the going was easier than it had been the day before.

A half a mile in, the pace slowed as the search intensified. Kal Cundiff and Mallory were several yards ahead of him; Kal searched the trail in front and to the left, Mallory to the right, while Annie bounded every which way and back and forth.

An hour in and his legs and feet had begun to ache. The going and having to test each step for trip and fall hazards were beginning to take their toll. By noon, his legs were on fire, but as far as he could tell, Mallory and even Kal seemed to be coping just fine.

By three, with the terrain steepening, he could go no further, so he called a halt and sat down on a fallen tree trunk.

Mallory, who'd said little to him for the last several hours, turned, came back and said, "You okay, Tucker?"

He shook his head and said, "No, not really. I'm sorry. I thought I was in good shape, but I'm just not used to this… to this. My legs are about to give out. If you don't mind, I'm going to sit here for a while. How far have we come?"

"Two and a half miles, maybe a bit more," she replied. "It's been slow going because of the search. D'you want to go back? The sheriff's party can't be far behind."

"We've been out here almost nine hours, Mallory," he said. "And we haven't found anything; no sign she was ever here. It's as if she disappeared off the planet."

Mallory nodded and sat down beside him. "You're right," she said. "I don't get it. I thought Annie would find something, but she hasn't. Not today or yesterday. Julie must have taken some other trail… I guess."

"Hey. Everything okay?" Kal asked. "We need to keep moving."

"You two go on," Tucker said. "You need to maintain the search. I'll sit—"

Kal's radio chirped. "This is Sheriff Cundiff, folks," he announced. "It's getting on for four, so I'm calling it a day. We'll pick up where we left off tomorrow, so group leaders, mark your spot and then make your way back to the trailhead, where there'll be some refreshments. Over and out."

Kal looked down at them and said, "You ready to go?"

"Give me a minute to get my breath, Deputy," Tucker said. "You go on ahead. I'll follow in a minute."

"I'll stay with him," Mallory said. "See you back at the cabin?"

Kal didn't look happy, but he nodded and said, "Be careful." Then he turned and walked away down the trail.

They sat there in silence for a moment until, unable to

stay quiet any longer, Mallory said, "What d'you think happened to her, Tucker? Be honest with me, okay?"

He took a deep breath, turned his head to look into her eyes and said, "I don't know, Mallory. I don't believe she fell off the trail into a gully. She's much too experienced to have done that, and I don't believe she took off either. There's something else in play. Either she was kidnapped, or…"

"Or she's dead," Mallory finished for him. "You think she's dead, too, don't you?"

He looked into her watery eyes and said, "That's what the odds are, I'm afraid. She's been gone nine days now… Look, there's a good chance she's been kidnapped. If so, we'll find her."

"Come on," Mallory said, standing up. "We've a long way to go. Here, let me help you up." She offered him her hand.

He was tempted to ignore it, but then, not wanting her to think he was being an ass, he reached up and took it, and she pulled him up. And, once again, he was impressed by her strength.

The trek back to the cabin was indeed long and, in the dim light, fraught with trip and fall hazards. But it was all downhill, and with Mallory leading the way, they made good time, though it was nearly eight-thirty and almost dark when they made it back to the ranger cabin. The cars and trucks were all gone, and the lot stood empty except for Mallory's car, Tucker's SUV, a single sheriff's cruiser and three ranger pickups.

"Let's sit a minute, shall we?" Mallory said.

She'd said little during the trek down the mountain. Tucker had assumed it was because she was concentrating on the trail, but little as he knew her, it seemed out of character. So, when she asked him to sit, he did. He sat down on the porch steps beside her. Annie jumped up, sat down beside him and pushed her head under his arm. He smiled and scratched her ears.

He glanced sideways at Mallory. She looked... defeated.

"...see you guys tomorrow," Kal said over his shoulder as he stepped out of the cabin. "Oh, hey, Mal, Mr. Randall. You made it then?"

She said nothing.

"Well," he said and paused for a second before continuing, "we didn't find anything, but that's a good thing, right?"

"Go away, Kal," she mumbled. Annie perked her head up and gave a little *yip*.

The deputy looked at Tucker and shrugged as if to say, *What can ya do?*

"You have a nice evening," he said, then walked down the steps and across the lot to his cruiser. And they watched as he drove out of the lot.

"You guys want some coffee?" Bert called from the open cabin door.

"Not me, thank you," Tucker said.

Mallory just shook her head.

"There was an awful lot of people turned up," she said, breaking the silence. "I was really surprised."

Tucker nodded. "Yeah, me too. It was a good effort."

"Can I be honest with you?" Mallory asked after a moment and then continued without waiting for an answer. "I don't know how I feel about today."

"What do you mean?" he asked.

She leaned back, pulled the scrunchie from her hair, shook her head and her blonde hair cascaded down around her shoulders.

"I'm frustrated, Tucker, and disappointed." She turned

her head to look at him. "We didn't find anything. All those people... dogs, horses, and cops... nothing."

"I know. I'm sorry," Tucker said quietly.

"But at the same time," she continued, "I'm relieved. You know? When the search began, I told myself I would be okay with whatever we found because at least I'd know. But as it progressed, and we got deeper into the woods, I kept thinking about it, and I... I began to pray we wouldn't find anything. How awful is that?" she asked.

Annie nudged him. He stroked her head.

"No, it's not awful. It's quite natural to feel that way," he replied. "Don't be so hard on yourself."

Mallory laughed, looked away and shook her head.

"What's so funny?" Tucker asked.

She turned her head and looked him in the eye. "Nothing," she said. "It's just that I can't believe you said that. I mean... People in glass houses."

Tucker frowned at her. "What's that supposed to mean?"

She rolled her eyes. "You're always so reserved," she said. "All that 'I work alone' stuff. I don't get it. Someone must have hurt you pretty badly."

"You've got to be kidding me," he said.

"Nope," she said. "I'm a pretty good judge of character. I haven't worked thirteen years in a bar for nothing. You want to talk about it?"

Tucker looked at his watch. It was just after nine. He looked up. The sky was a field of stars. He looked to the east. In the glow of the lights of Cleveland, Tennessee, some thirty-five miles away to the west, he could see what looked like gathering storm clouds, though it wasn't supposed to rain again for several days.

He glanced at her. She was still staring at him. And suddenly, he felt uncomfortable.

"That's not a good idea," he answered eventually. "It's getting late and..."

She nodded. "I have a question. You don't have to answer if you don't want to, but when I was talking to Sheriff Cundiff, you were looking at your phone. What was that all about? Were you avoiding me? Why would you do that?"

Tucker took a deep breath, not quite knowing how to answer.

"This is your big chance, Agent Randall," David Lewis said. "SAIC isn't a fancy title. It's the real thing, and you earned it. And the Clines are old friends. I'd hate for anything to happen. But I really think you're ready for this."

"I am, sir!" Tucker replied. "I won't let you down."

"And I have every confidence in you," David said.

Marsha Cline had been working as a waitress—a temporary job between semesters in college—when one of her customers forgot to take their credit card. She'd rushed out to find the woman but had heard sounds of a struggle in the alley beside the restaurant. As she went to investigate, a man came running out, bumped into her, looked her in the eyes, and then shoved her aside and bolted. Marsha looked down the alley and saw a man lying on the ground. She ran to him. She was going to help him to his feet, but he'd been stabbed several times. She called 911, but by the time the ambulance arrived, he'd bled out and was dead.

Marsha had witnessed a murder, the latest in a line of unsolved stabbings. She was the only witness who could identify the killer.

Two days later, the restaurant was broken into, and the employee files stolen. The next day, two of the restaurant employees were stabbed to death. So the Clines had sought out David Lewis, and he had appointed Tucker to watch the young woman.

He sighed and said, "I wasn't avoiding you, Mallory. I

CHAPTER 14

found an old picture on my phone, one I thought I'd deleted a long time ago. It's the picture of a young woman I was assigned to protect... It ended badly."

He took out his phone and found the picture of himself with David Lewis standing next to an older couple. And between the couple...

"Oh... my God. That looks like Julie!" Mallory gasped.

"I know," Tucker said. "That's Marsha Cline. That's who I was supposed to protect. She was a witness in the biggest case in my FBI career five years ago. She was frightened, but between me and her parents... We, that is I, persuaded her to testify against a murderer."

She bit her bottom lip as she looked at him, wide-eyed.

"My boss," he continued, "assured me, and her, that she'd be safe, that she'd be protected, but..." His voice broke.

"You don't have to go on," Mallory said.

Tucker continued anyway, "But he was wrong. I persuaded her. I took her statement. She described the killer perfectly. But..." He let out a sigh. "It turned out the case was bigger than we all thought. What she saw was a mob execution, and the police had busted a major drug operation. Less than twenty-four hours after she'd identified the killer, she was dead."

"That was not your fault," Mallory said firmly. "You can't blame yourself."

He looked sideways at her, smiled grimly and said, "Who else is to blame? The killer? My boss? Her parents? No. I was the one who handled it wrong, and she paid for it with her life." *That she did, Tucker*—it was an angry whisper at the back of his mind—*and I'm never going to let you forget it.*

"When your sister and Jared arrived in my office," he continued, "I'd already made up my mind to take a case in

Nebraska. I was... I was just humoring them, but then Jennifer showed me a photo of Julie and I thought I was seeing a ghost."

"Tucker," Mallory said. "I'm sorry. I had no idea."

Tucker, feeling embarrassed that he'd confessed so much to a woman he hardly knew, stood up to leave. But Mallory stood too, placing herself in front of him, her eyes filled with tears.

"Thank you for taking our case. I know how hard it must have been for you. I wonder if... But shouldn't we get going?"

He smiled at her and said, "Yes, we should. We have another long day tomorrow."

"You're right," she said. "Of course, you are. I'll see you tomorrow then. Have a good night, Tucker." And she turned and walked to her car.

"Mallory," he called after her.

She turned, her hand on the handle of her car door and looked at him, "Yes?"

"What did you want to ask me?"

She paused, frowned, thought for a moment, then said, "I don't remember. It couldn't have been important. Goodnight, Tucker."

She turned to her car, opened the door for Annie to jump in, climbed in after her and drove away into the night.

"Goodnight, Mallory," he muttered as he watched her go.

15

FRIDAY THROUGH MONDAY

Mallory, unhappy with the way the search the previous day had turned out, decided to organize her own search party: Jennifer and Jared, with Jacqueline—Julie's elder sister. They would be taking Jared's Gator 4x4. Sarah Alexander —Julie's best friend—was also joining them with a handful of their former classmates. But not Tucker Randall.

It had been around five-thirty that morning when she called him.

"Hey," she said when he answered. "You still in bed?"

"No, I woke early. I'm in the kitchen making coffee… Look, Mallory, I hope you'll forgive me, but I'm not going to be able to make it today. My legs and hips have stiffened up, and I can barely walk. I should have known better. So, I'll just stay in my office today. I have plenty of research and investigating on Julie's case to do. And you have to admit that I wasn't much help yesterday."

"Oh, I wouldn't say that," she replied, "but I do understand, and, yes, you should stay home and rest for at least a couple of days. I've organized a search party of my own. We're going to search the Ridge Trail, which is probably a waste of time. I don't see her going all the way up there, but you never know, and it will keep me away from Kal's groping fingers."

"Well, you know where I am," he said. "Please let me know if you find anything."

"You bet. You rest up, okay? Talk to you later, Tucker." And she hung up, feeling a little disappointed he wasn't going to join her.

The next three days passed slowly and fruitlessly.

On day one, they found nothing at all. The second day, they found the remains of a campsite—a stone fire ring, some scraps of fabric perhaps from a tent, some empty food cans, beer cans, bottles, and other trash. On the third day, they found a small cabin. There was no one there, but there were signs of recent habitation: cans of food, bottles of water, some pieces of paper—notes, sketches, doodles—ashes in the fireplace, and an iron bed with a mattress and a couple of blankets. Other than that, nothing.

The sheriff's department sent a CSI unit to investigate both sites, but neither one yielded any indication Julie had ever been there.

And so it went on to the point where Mallory found herself praying that Julie was dead, because if she wasn't, if she was alive, what would it mean? *If she's been abducted? What horrible things are they doing to her?*

On day four of the search—now without most of Julie's former classmates or Jared because of his limitations—Mallory was wondering why they hadn't seen anything of Zach Burns. Howie O'Neal said he lived up that way in an old cabin, and she wondered if it was the one they'd found. She knew, of course, there were several more cabins scattered around the forest, but it was possible. *But where is he? He has to be somewhere, right?*

She'd talked to Tucker on the phone several times during the four days, but he'd had nothing constructive to say. And, truth be told, neither had she.

Mallory had also been talking back and forth with Julie's friends, trying to figure out what they were missing, because there had to be something. But they had nothing helpful to add, and she felt as if she'd run into a brick wall.

She also had a feeling that if she and Tucker could put their heads together, maybe they could figure out what it was she was missing.

As she was getting ready to go to work that Monday afternoon, Mallory couldn't help but think of some of the more perplexing true crime cases that she'd heard about. She wondered how the smooth voice of Dark Tidings would handle Julie's tale…

Tragedy struck the small, upscale community just beyond the city limits of Chattanooga when a young woman seemingly disappeared, vanished without a trace. Julie Romero—twenty-three—a sociable young woman whose smile could light up any room, was an experienced hunting guide who loved the outdoors until… a routine hiking trip in the Cherokee National Forest turned into what appears to be an unsolvable mystery. No evidence as to how or why she disappeared has ever been—

Mallory shook her head and forced herself to focus on the task at hand, but then, *No,* she thought, *that's not going to happen. The police may have ended the search, but they haven't closed the case. And Tucker is still here, and I know he's cracked tougher cases than this one.*

"Vinnie, I'm here," she called as she walked into The Saloon.

She felt nauseous. She was tired. No, she was worn out and wished to hell she could take some time off, but she needed the money; it was the only thing keeping her afloat, both financially and mentally. And it was the single constant in the ever-evolving catastrophe that had suddenly become her life.

Maybe you wouldn't be so tired and nauseous if you ate properly, a voice in the back of her head said, a ghostly version of Jennifer's nagging rhetoric. She pursed her lips, knowing it was true. She hadn't eaten a proper meal since the pizza she'd enjoyed with Tucker.

Vinnie called over from the jukebox, "You wanna try fixing this piece of junk? I been at it all day."

"Sure, Vinnie," she said and sighed.

"And while you're doing it, don't forget to mind the bar," he added.

"Sure, Vinnie," she repeated, too tired to argue.

"What? Is there an echo in here?" Vinnie said as he shuffled off to his office.

For several minutes, she tried to figure out what was wrong with the ancient jukebox but gave up in frustration. *The poor thing has run its course,* she thought. *We should take it out back and shoot it, put it out of its misery.*

She went behind the bar and began to clean up Vinnie's mess and, out of habit, she stuck an earbud into her left ear, covered it with her hair, and turned on a Dark Tidings podcast. But after a few minutes of listening to Devin Rudd talk about how Lawrence Bittaker abducted one of his victims, she shut it off. Every word sounded like a description of what might have happened to Julie, and she just couldn't stomach it anymore.

Her stomach was churning, reminding her she'd eaten

only a slice of toast and apple all day. She looked around the bar. There were only six customers and, of course, Art Peters, who was in his usual spot propping up the end of the bar. Everyone's glasses or bottles seemed to be full so, after a final glance at the old machine—*he could replace it for a hundred bucks,* she fumed—she went to the back room and turned on the air fryer.

Vinnie didn't have much of a selection. The only reason he'd bought the machine was an attempt to compete with an Applebee's-wannabe just up the road. His selection of overpriced appetizers was scraped from the bottom shelf of a convenience store freezer section he'd picked up at a sale.

She sighed and set a fish filet, chicken nuggets and some mozzarella sticks to cook for fifteen minutes and then went back out to "mind the bar."

In the forty-five minutes since she'd been at work, no one had entered, and only one person had left.

As she waited for her food to cook, she looked out over the bar at the five patrons scattered around the room, three in one booth, one in another, and another at a table, plus Art at the end of the bar, but he didn't count. He was a fixture.

Why do they come here to drink alone? she wondered.

The timer in the back room dinged, and she went back to find her food burned on one side. *Idiot!* she chided herself. *You were supposed to flip them halfway.* She started rummaging through the freezer for more, but Vinnie poked his head out of the office.

"Hey, what you doing?"

"I burned my food," she explained. "I'm going to make another plate."

"You make another plate, you're going to pay for it, right?"

"Oh, come on, Vinnie, look at this?" She showed him her fish filet. "I can't eat that."

"You should pay more attention. You get one meal a shift, and you're lucky I give you that. You think I'm made of money?"

"And I hardly ever take it!" she said. "So, you're saying you'll charge me for cooking tomorrow's meal?"

"Not if you make it tomorrow!" he said and pulled his head back into the office.

I should just throw this crap at him, she thought as she turned everything over and ran the air fryer for a few more minutes. *That's the way to do it. Scrape off the black and use lots of sauce... What a dickhead.*

After a long and boring shift of filling the glasses of the few customers she had, she looked at the clock to find it was still only ten o'clock. Art had gone home early for a change, and the last customer had walked out fifteen minutes earlier, and she doubted there'd be anyone else coming in, so she went back to the office.

"Vinnie, it's been dead all night," she said. "There's no one out there, not even Art, so is it okay if I leave early?"

"What you want to leave for?" he asked. "Your shift is to eleven. You can stand out there and get paid for doing nothing, right? Put on your scary stories and ride my dime."

"Oh, come on, Vinnie, I'm exhausted. I've spent almost two weeks trying to do something about Julie."

"Yeah," he agreed. "You get up stupid early, run around all morning, then come in tired and complain about it. I noticed."

She resisted the urge to slap him for his lack of empathy. "Well, I want to go home and go to bed. Get some rest, and come in fresh tomorrow." Every word was a lie, but she expected he knew that.

"Whatever." He waved a hand dismissively at her. "I wouldn't do this for Roger or Patty. But you're my best bartender. Go on. Piss off and get some rest." And with that, he turned back to his ancient computer.

And so Mallory drove home. The ride was uneventful, but try as she might, she couldn't get Julie out of her mind.

Fifteen minutes after she left The Saloon, she entered her house, let Annie out the back door and poured herself a large glass of red. That done, she picked up her flashlight and wandered out into the dark, down the paved path to the fence at the end of her backyard.

It was a moonless night, the air humid, the sky a vast field of stars, though storm clouds were gathering to the west and she could feel rain in the air.

She stood at the fence and stared at the silhouette of the distant mountains to the east, dark against the indigo sky, and her heart went out to Julie. *Where are you, Jules? Where the hell are you?*

She heard something snap. In the quiet of the night, it sounded like a gunshot. She looked to her left but could see only the outline of the tall trees that separated her lot from the one next door.

Snap!

Oh, m'God. There it is again. A gun. Her heart hammered in her chest. *I should have brought a gun. Why didn't I bring a gun? I have a gun! Why didn't I bring a gun!*

Another snap, this one much closer.

"Annie," she whispered. "Where are you?" But Annie wasn't there. She was off somewhere, out in the field beyond the fence, *schnauzing for rabbits, no doubt*, she thought.

She spun around, terrified that she was about to come face to face with... what? She didn't know. She waved her flashlight this way and that, and then... she found herself looking into the bearded face of a man.

Shocked, she stumbled backward into the fence, almost falling, but before she could hit the ground, the man reached out, grabbed her arm and, without saying a word, pulled her to her feet.

"Julie?" The voice was deep, dry, questioning.

"What? Who are you? What do you know about Julie?" she whispered, her voice shaking.

The shadowy figure cocked his head to one side. All she could see under his hood were his eyes, glinting darkly. "Mallory?" the voice sounded somehow less frightening and... familiar.

"Who are you?" she said, her voice rising in volume. "What d'you know about Julie? Tell me, please."

But instead of answering, the man backed away, then turned and ran.

"Please," she yelled. "Don't go. Tell me about Julie. Come back. I need to know!"

But all was still and quiet as the tears rolled down her cheeks. She bent down, picked up the flashlight, and started back along the path to her back deck, where she sat down, her empty, forgotten glass in one hand, her flashlight in the other, and began to cry loudly.

Five minutes later, Annie came bounding along the path and up onto the deck.

"Where've you been, you little monster?" she said, reaching out to fondle the dog's head. "Fat lot of good you are. I could have been murdered and you wouldn't have known."

16

FRIDAY EVENING 11PM

Tucker had spent the four days at his office, at the police department, the local sheriff's office and even the Hamilton County sheriff's department digging through old files and folders. To say he'd worn out his welcome would be the understatement of the century; to the point where Sheriff Cundiff was tempted to throw him out.

He searched through every file box he could find, every case file on the departmental computers, anything to do with missing persons, smuggling and forest-related crimes.

He'd visited the library and used their microfiche reader—*Microfiche! Really?*—to search old newspapers for any hints or clues, even speculations about any series of related crimes in the area. He'd even attempted to interview some of the older folks in Benton, Copper Hill and Ducktown, but no one would talk, especially when they realized he was looking into local crime.

So, that Monday afternoon, Tucker was mentally

exhausted and reduced to sitting at his desk staring up at the ceiling.

"I just don't understand it, Debbie," he said, though he suspected it wasn't the first time he'd said it. "Why did the dog get left behind?"

"I don't know, sir," Debbie replied.

"I mean, Tobin was Julie's dog, right? If she was planning to do a runner, she wouldn't have left him behind, would she?"

"No, sir. Did she always take the dog with her?" Debbie asked.

"As far as I know, yes. So, if she left the dog, she didn't leave town, and something bad must have happened to her."

The vet had given Tobin the all-clear, and he was back with the Romeros. *Maybe Mallory's idea about taking him up the trail is a good one.*

And then there's the missing Ford Bronco. Hah! Scrapyards. That's another lead that hasn't been followed up on. He did a quick search online and found no less than a dozen salvage yards in Hamilton County alone. Five in Bradley County and several dozen more spread out over a dozen Southeast Tennessee counties.

"Hey, Debbie," he said, "I need you to do something for me. I need—"

"Mr. Randall?" she said. "It's almost seven o'clock."

He blinked twice, then looked at his watch. It was indeed almost seven.

"I'm really sorry, sir," she said. "I know you like me to stay late sometimes, but I really do need to get home tonight. Ben made a roast today, and he's expecting me."

"Of course, Debbie," he said. "I'm sorry. I wasn't paying attention to the time. Go on home and enjoy your dinner.

What I need will wait until tomorrow. We'll talk about it in the morning."

"Thank you, Mr. Randall," she said and collected her things. "See you in the morning, then. D'you want me to come in early?"

"No. Eight-thirty will be fine."

She closed the door and Tucker leaned back in his chair, linked his fingers behind his head and closed his eyes. It was quiet; too quiet.

"Maybe I should get myself a dog," he mused. "Someone to talk to when it gets lonely in here."

He looked at his watch again. It was fifteen after seven; too late to call the salvage yards, so he buried himself in copies of crime reports going back over the last twenty years. *If I don't get a break soon, I'm going to have to refund the Romeros. Okay, so where's the Bronco? If we can find it, it would be a solid lead.*

At a little after nine, he tossed the fruitless crime reports aside and turned to Mallory's maps and compared them to copies of the maps they'd used during the searches. There were some slight differences between them, but he ascribed that to different hands tracing them out. He looked at copies of the notes Sheriff Cundiff had made. Comparing those to the maps, he was pretty sure most of the trails over a ten-mile radius had been well-explored. Yes, there were several spidery-looking, unexplored squiggles on Mallory's map which he thought might be worth a look, but—

And that was the last he remembered until he was awakened by a mighty banging on the front door that startled him awake. His chin cupped in his palm, he jerked but caught himself and rubbed his face. *What time is it? Five after eleven! Geez. How long have I been asleep?*

He looked down at his desk. He'd switched from Mallory's maps to Julie's bank statements and then to her text messages, hoping to find any connection.

The banging continued. *What the hell?* He rose to his feet, went to the door and opened it to find a rain-soaked Mallory Carver.

She pushed past him into the room and turned to face him, her arms thrust down by her sides. "I know that this isn't the best time, but I've been attacked. Well, not actually attacked, but I was at the bottom of my yard and there was a man. He had a beard and... Tucker, he *scared* me, and I fell, and he grabbed me and then—"

"Whoa, stop," he interrupted. "Is he still there?" *Stupid question. Of course he isn't.*

She paused, shook her head and said, "No."

"Well just hold on. You're soaking wet. I'll get you some towels." He went into the house and returned a moment later with several bath towels and handed them to her.

"When did it start raining?" he asked.

"I don't know. Not long ago. Twenty minutes, maybe?"

"Get yourself dried off," he said. "I'll go get some blankets." She nodded.

"Feel better now?" he asked after she'd wrapped herself up and sat down on the couch.

Again, she nodded, staring at him.

"So," he said, "are you going to tell me about it?"

She looked up at him and said, "I'm sorry. I didn't know what else to do."

"Tell me what happened."

"Well, Vinnie let me off work early, and I went home and let Annie out, then I went to get some air. I walked to the fence at the end of my property to look at the mountains and..."

"You said someone grabbed you," Tucker said. "Who was it?"

"I... I don't know for sure," she replied. "But I think it might have been Zach Burns."

"What?" Tucker frowned. "You mean the kid who killed his mother?"

"I don't know. It was dark. He was wearing a hoodie and he had a beard. He only said two words. 'Julie?' a question, as if he thought I was her. Then he recognized me and said 'Mallory.' It was when he said my name that I thought I recognized his voice."

"And he didn't say anything else?" Tucker said thoughtfully.

"No. I asked him what he knew about her, but he didn't answer. He just backed away, then turned and ran. He was big, Tucker; huge."

She paused for a second, then said, "Maybe I am making too much of this. What could have—"

"No, no," Tucker interrupted. "This could be the break we've been looking for. We need to find this guy. If he's who you think he is and he thought you were Julie, it means he didn't kill her. This guy O'Neal you told me about. He said Burns was living in a cabin somewhere up there in the forest. D'you know where it is?"

"No," she replied, "but I do know where Howie lives. First thing in the morning, I'll go there and ask him."

"I think I'll join you," Tucker said. "I was going to start looking for the Bronco at the salvage yards, but my assistant can start researching that for me. Are you hungry? Would you like something to eat?"

"No... Well, maybe a little? I burned my dinner at Vinnie's place. It was awful."

"Hang tight, then. I'll go make you something hot."

"That would be wonderful. Thank you," she replied.

When he returned less than ten minutes later with a

plate of lasagna, he found her stretched out on the couch, fast asleep.

17

SATURDAY MORNING 7AM

Mallory woke with a start, sat up and looked around. *Oh my God,* she thought. *I'm in Tucker's office. Oh crap. This is terrible. What was I thinking? I have to get out of here before—*

"Oh, you're up. Would you like some coffee?"

Crap! she thought as she turned her head to look at him.

He was standing in the doorway, leaning against the frame with his arms folded, smiling down at her.

Inwardly, she shook her head, sighed and accepted the situation for what it was; bad.

"Yes. Please," she said. "But first, I need to go out to my car and grab my purse."

"If there's anything you need to clean up or whatever, you only have to just ask," he replied.

"I appreciate the gesture," she said, "but I'm pretty sure you don't have anything a woman carries in her purse." And she immediately regretted her choice of words. *Damn! Now I sound like I'm— Oh hell, what does it matter? I must look like hell.*

"Tucker," she said. "I need to go home. I need a shower, a change of clothes, and, and I need that coffee, please."

"By all means," he replied easily. "You can take a shower here. You can... borrow one of my T-shirts. We can eat some breakfast, and then we'll go to your place. You can change clothes, and then we'll head out to see this Howie guy. Okay?"

"I guess," she said, "but coffee first."

"Yes, ma'am," he replied. "Right this way, if you please."

And she stood and followed him into the kitchen.

It was just after nine that morning when Tucker turned off Tennessee 30 in Greasy Creek onto the dirt road that led to the log house where Howie O'Neal lived alone with three coonhounds.

He parked the car next to Howie's pickup, and he and Mallory stepped out to be immediately surrounded by the three friendly dogs, all woofing excitedly and wagging their tails.

The day was warm, but with a slight breeze wafting through the trees. Howie's cabin—a modern, polished log build set on two acres of woodland—was not quite next door to another, much older cabin surrounded by a couple of dozen vehicles in various stages of disrepair: some on blocks, some on flat tires, some almost swallowed by long grass and creepers, and all dated earlier than 1970. The lot was a veritable graveyard: the place where unloved classic cars go to die.

"What's with that one?" Tucker asked, nodding at the dilapidated cabin.

"It's an old homesteading thing," Mallory replied. "It belongs to Howie, too. Dates back to the early nineteen hundreds. You find a spot, chop down a few trees, build yourself a cabin, then, many years later, when you've had time to build a decent house, you turn the old homestead into a handy outbuilding. Smoke meats, store vegetables, cure tobacco, keep animals, whatever your fancy. That one looks to be about... I dunno. Maybe sixty years or so old? It's... kinda nostalgic, don't you think?"

She pointed a little further away. "See that bald patch of ground over there? That looks like the location of the original cabin. That pile of rocks looks like it might have been the chimney or maybe a burn spot. Or maybe it was a garden. It's hard to say anymore. They would have used what was left of the structure as firewood to heat the new cabin in winter."

She glanced at Tucker and saw him nodding, putting it together in his mind.

"You really know this stuff, don't you?" he asked.

She smiled at him but said nothing.

"Hey, little girl, whatchu think you're doin' sneaking about on my property?" Howie O'Neal said from the front porch.

"Sneaking?" she replied. "A bear makes less noise chasing down a deer."

"Ain't that the truth," he grumbled. "I heard ya comin' from more'n a quarter mile away."

"As intended," Mallory said. "Everyone knows you don't sneak onto a man's property around here. That will get you shot in a hurry."

"Ain't that the truth?" Howie repeated. "So watcha doin' here?"

"Mr. O'Neal, I'd like to ask you a few questions, if I may —" Tucker began.

"Nope! Ya may not." Howie turned to Mallory. "But the lady has my attention."

"You mentioned Zach Burns the last time we spoke," Mallory said, inwardly smiling. "You said he lives in a cabin somewhere up here. D'you know where, exactly?"

"Sure do," he replied.

"Oh good," Mallory said, taking her map from her pocket. "Could you show me where it is on this map?"

"Gimme that thing." He held out his hand and she stepped forward and handed it to him.

"So it's right around here somewhere… just above this ridge right here," Howie said, pointing to a spot on the map.

"Is there an easy way to get there?" she asked. "Can we drive?"

"Sure, sure," he replied. "You need to drive on up this road right here"—he traced the route with his finger—"for maybe two-and-half miles, then you make another right here and drive on for maybe another mile, and it'll be on your right. The number's one-oh-five, if I remember c'rectly. There's a mailbox at the entrance to a dirt driveway. Drive on up there to the cabin. It's quite a way…" He paused for a moment, looked her in the eyes and continued, "Now, you take care up there, missy. It's wild country, and that boy ain't quite right in the head, if you know what I mean."

"Thank you, Howie," she said. "You're a treasure." And she leaned in and kissed him on the cheek.

"Well, I'll be," he said, putting his hand to his cheek. "You get on outa here, you young hussy," he said, smiling.

Ten minutes later, deep in the forest, Mallory, glad she wasn't alone, stopped the car in front of a dilapidated mailbox upon which she could barely make out the number 105; the paint weathered and faint.

"This is it, Tucker," she said. "Howie was right when he said it was a dirt road," she continued as she gazed at the

CHAPTER 17

overgrown entrance to the driveway. Had she not been looking for it, she would undoubtedly have passed it by without even knowing it was there.

She backed up a little, turned into the driveway and drove on up the hill, the overhanging branches brushing the sides and roof of the car.

After what had to have been several hundred yards, she broke out into a small clearing in the middle of which was a long, low log-built cabin surrounded by a wraparound porch. The house itself was surrounded by a lawn, surprisingly well-manicured.

She drove on up to the house and parked beside a dilapidated 1970s Ford F-150.

She sat for a moment, staring up at the front door. Despite her confidence and knowing that she had Tucker with her, she felt infinitely nervous about confronting the man who had frightened her so badly only a few hours earlier.

"Mallory, are you okay?" Tucker asked, and for a moment, she wanted to tell him she wasn't.

"I can do this," he said. "You don't need to…"

Oh no. It's on, now, she thought and, seizing upon a rush of bravado, she unbuckled her seat belt, saying, "Nope, I'm going to do this. Besides, if he hurt you, I'd never forgive myself."

"Him? Hurt me?" Tucker said, grinning as he pulled his jacket open to reveal the Glock 17 in its holster under his left arm. "They don't call me 'Quick Draw McGraw' for nothing. I'm ex-FBI, remember?"

"Geez," she said, shaking her head. "All right. Let's do this." And she pushed the door open and stepped out of the car. She was about to mount the steps when she heard something behind her.

"What're you doing here?" a voice snarled. "Don't you know you're trespassin'?"

Mallory jumped, startled, and whirled around.

Tucker, half out the passenger door, true to his word, in one smooth action, swept his right hand under his jacket and pulled the Glock. *Oh, m'God. How did he do that?* she wondered.

Twenty yards away, on the edge of the trees, stood a bearded man aiming a compound hunting bow at them, the bowstring pulled taut.

"Put the bow down, Zach," Tucker said quietly, just loud enough for the man to hear.

"I said, what're you doing here? This is private property," the large man shouted.

"We've come to talk to you, Zach," Mallory said calmly, though she was on the verge of panic. "It's me, Mallory. You came to my house last night. You knew who I was then."

The large man held the bow steady but didn't reply.

"Tucker, put the gun away. I can handle him," she said quietly, trying not to tremble.

"Mallory, we—"

"—are trespassing," she finished for him.

Tucker did as he was asked and holstered the weapon.

"Zach," Mallory said, "You came to my house last night. You were looking for Julie. Please, can we talk about it?"

Slowly, the bearded man lowered the bow and slackened the string.

"You're Zach Burns," she said. "We were at school together. Don't you remember?"

He nodded. "I remember. Why're you here?"

"You thought I was Julie... Zach, could we sit down somewhere to talk?" she asked.

CHAPTER 17

Burns thought about it for a moment, then walked over to them, the bow at his side in his right hand.

He marched past them, up the steps, took a keyring from his left pants pocket and unlocked the door. Then turned and said, "Come on." And he disappeared inside.

Tucker looked at Mallory and said, "Well, you did say he was big."

18

SATURDAY MORNING 11AM

And Zach Burns was indeed a big man. Tucker estimated he had to be at least six-four. At six-one and broad-shouldered, and with his FBI training, Tucker had always figured he was a match for just about anyone; but this guy? He was a bear of a man.

They followed him inside and watched as he hung the bow over the fireplace.

He turned to face them, looked at them and said, "Don't entertain much. You want some tea?"

Tucker was about to decline, but he saw Mallory give him a look, so he changed his mind and said, "Sure. Please. Thank you."

"Me too, please, Zach," Mallory said.

Zach Burns went to the refrigerator and returned with a jug of golden-green liquid and poured some of it into two skinny tumblers.

That's a pitcher and two bar glasses! she thought.

"I make it myself," he said as he placed them on the

table. "The leaves grow on the south side of the mountain. There's an old cottage there. Nobody goes there anymore, only me. Sit down, why don't ya?"

They sat down at the table. Burns remained standing.

Tucker picked up his glass and took a sip, then looked at Burns in surprise. "This is excellent," he said. "What is it?"

"It's tea with some herbs from the old cottage garden."

"It's wonderful," Mallory said. "Zach, you should sell this."

"Hah! No one would buy from me," Zach said. "All they can think about is my momma."

After that there was a moment of strained silence until, finally, Tucker said, "We're here to talk about Julie Romero, Zach. She's been missing for two weeks. We think she got lost somewhere in the forest. We were hoping you might know something or may even have heard something."

"Julie?" The name rolled off his tongue. "You know better than that, Mallory," he said as he sat down at the table. "Julie would never get lost around here."

"Well, do you have any idea what might have happened to her?" Tucker asked.

He shook his head. "I know she's nice," he said. "She comes around here most weeks. Sometimes she stops and we talk."

"She went missing on the thirteenth," Tucker persisted. "D'you know anything about that, Zach?"

The big man's eyes narrowed. He looked angry. "What are you sayin'? You think I had somethin' to do with it? No! I don't know what happened to her. I was looking for her last night. I thought you were her," he said, looking at Mallory.

Tucker was about to say something more, but Mallory

cut in and said, "What about her dog, Zach? What about Tobin? Did you see him?"

"Yeah, I've seen him, Toby. In the woods with Julie. Then he was here, by himself, all alone. I tried to give him some food, but he just growled at me and ran away. That's why I was lookin' for Julie last night. I knew something was wrong." He looked down at the table, utterly downcast.

"So, when was the last time you saw him without Julie?"

Zach was silent, then looked down and away to his left, a sure sign he was about to lie, but he didn't; he looked up at them and didn't answer.

"All right," Tucker said, changing the subject. "You seem to know the woods pretty well. Have you any idea where she might have gone? Is there anywhere, any trail that the search parties might have missed?"

"Search parties?" Zach looked confused at first. "Oh, yeah. I saw them stumbling around out there."

"And," Tucker kept his tone neutral. "Did they miss anything, d'you think?"

Zach laughed. It sounded weird, like a cross between a dog bark and a seagull cawing.

"They kept to the main trails; missed more'n half the branches, the small trails. I did see you out there a couple of times, Mallory. You walked some of them, but the police and the Feds… they don't know these woods as well as they'd like you to believe. They didn't go nowhere near the trails Julie walks."

"What about the other people who live on the mountain?" Mallory asked, "The 'shiners, the pot farmers. Heck, even the pagans. D'you think Julie might have upset any of them?"

"No." He shook his head. "Most of them stay away from the townies, and as for the witches, they only come by in spring an' fall. All they do is dance an' stuff, an' drink themselves stupid. They make fires. The forest service keeps an eye on them and shuts them down during fire season. They're harmless."

Tucker frowned. None of what he was hearing came together, considering what he'd heard said about this man. *He's been living alone too long, but he's as sane as I am,* he thought. *Mallory said there's a rumor he killed his mother but was never convicted. I'm not seeing it.*

"When was the last time you talked to Julie, Zach?" he asked.

"Huh." Zach was quiet for a few moments, then frowned and said, "Must have been the day before I saw Toby wanderin' around on his own. Didn't get to talk to her much. She was with her friend."

"With her friend?" Mallory said, raising her voice. "What friend? Are you talking about Sarah?"

"Sarah. Yeah. She wanted Sarah to meet me. She talked about it a lot before she brought her. She said it was important. I don't think she liked me."

Mallory was about to speak, but before she could, Tucker held up a hand, stopped her, and said, "Why was it important, Zach?"

Burns looked at him but didn't say anything.

"Zach! Why did Julie say it was important?" Mallory demanded.

Again he looked away to the left, then said, "I'm not gonna say," he replied sullenly.

"Tell me what she said," Mallory said angrily.

"I'm not supposed to tell anyone," Zach said, his brow furrowed. "You need to go now."

"Oh no," she snapped. "That's not how it works, Zach. You're going to tell me what you know, and you're going to tell me now."

CHAPTER 18

Burns stood up, his face red with anger. "Get outta my house," he growled. "And don't come back."

Tucker stood, grabbed Mallory by her arm and pulled her to her feet. "Come on. We need to go." Then he turned to Burns, held up both of his hands and said, "It's okay, Zach. Just calm down. We're leaving."

"But—" Mallory said as he grabbed her arm again and steered her across the room.

"Shush," Tucker said as he opened the door.

Once inside the truck, Mallory sat still, staring up at the door, a single tear rolling down her cheek.

"Hey, hey," Tucker said. "It's okay."

"I'm sorry," she said and wiped her cheek with the back of her hand. "I really screwed that up, didn't I? Now he'll never talk to us again. What if he's the only person who can help?"

Tucker, trying not to think about that, said, "Well, we now know a lot more than we did. We know Julie was friendly with Burns, and we know she introduced him to her friend Sarah. I know you must have talked to her. She was part of your search party, wasn't she? Did she mention meeting Burns?"

Mallory slowly shook her head. "No. She didn't. But you're right," she said. "He said he saw Julie and Sarah the day before he saw Tobin alone. That means—"

"—that Sarah could have been the last person to see Julie alive," Tucker finished for her.

Mallory's face hardened. She grabbed a tissue from the center console and wiped her eyes. "I've read their texts, and I talked to her myself," she muttered. "And she never said a thing. We need to talk to her."

She flashed her keys at him. "And I know exactly where the pony princess is going to be today."

She stuffed the key into the ignition, turned it, the

engine fired, and Mallory reversed away from Zach's front porch, made a turn and drove back down the long, narrow driveway.

Five minutes later, they were back on Tennessee 30 heading for Highway 64 with Tucker holding onto the strap above his door as Mallory drove the pickup over the bumps and potholes. Finally, she made a hard right onto Highway 64, and Tucker heaved a sigh of relief and let go of the strap. He glanced at her several times as they headed back toward Chattanooga, but her eyes remained focused straight ahead until they hit APD 40 and then I-75 south. Only then did Mallory let up and relax a little.

"The Alexanders are one of the wealthiest families in Hamilton County," Mallory said, finally breaking the silence as she hurtled up Whiteoak Mountain at eighty miles an hour. "No one knows who owns more land around here, them or the Burns family; Zach's folks. Old man Alexander owns CKD Chemicals. It's old money."

"Where do the Burns get their money?" Tucker asked.

"Real estate," she replied. "They own half of downtown... Well, not half, but a lot. Anyway, Sarah's always been into horses. She plays polo, you know."

"She doesn't sound much like Julie at all," Tucker said. "Strange bedfellows. How come they're so close?"

Mallory laughed and shook her head. "They've been buddies since... I don't know when. They were the two chirpiest kindergartners you ever did see. They latched on to each other from the outset and never let go."

She drove on in silence for the next several minutes, then took the Ooltewah exit and said, "We're almost there. How are we going to handle it?"

"There's no getting around it," Tucker said. "She has some answering to do. There's no point in trying to sugarcoat it. We'll just dive right in and ask the questions."

"Right," Mallory said, nodding. "Right," she muttered, more to herself than to Tucker.

Five minutes later, she pulled off the road and onto a paved drive bounded by an avenue of neatly trimmed trees that gave way to a vast open area at the far end of which was a huge, three-story mansion flanked on one side by a six-car garage and on the other by a matching atrium. To the rear and to the right, Tucker could see a horse barn that was almost as big as the house, surrounded by what he knew to be horse training rings—some with jumps, some without. The complex portrayed the image of wealth on a grand scale, and Tucker could only gawk at the layout in amazement.

Beyond the barn, in one of the rings, several people were watching a rider putting a beautiful black horse through its paces, leaping over one jump after another until finally, it galloped like a wild thing for the gate while the watchers stood and clapped.

"That's Sarah," Mallory said. "They say she could have made the US Olympic Equestrian Team but didn't have the b... But she backed out during the trials. She's pretty damn good though," she finished a little wistfully.

By then they were at the barn and out of the car, and the rider noticed them and waved, then she turned, leaned down and said something to several of the watchers who turned and looked at them, and then she rode across the field to join them.

"That's a black Friesian," Mallory said as the horse and rider approached. "They're not great jumpers, but they are beautiful. Must have cost them a fortune."

"How d'you know that?" Tucker asked. "D'you ride?"

"Me? Hell no. I could never afford it. No, I'm just a mine of worthless information, as they say."

Tucker stared at the horse's rippling muscles, its

gleaming coat, and its easy gait in awe. It looked as if it had leapt off the cover of a book.

"You're right," he said. "It's beautiful."

"Hi, Mallory," Sarah said. "How are you holding up?"

"As well as can be expected, I guess," she replied. "This is Tucker Randall. He's the private investigator Jennifer hired to find Julie. Tucker, this is Sarah Alexander."

"Nice to meet you," Sarah said.

"Likewise," Tucker replied. "That's a beautiful horse."

She leaned forward and patted the animal's neck. The horse tossed its head, shook it, and then whinnied.

"Thank you," Sarah said.

"Good jumper?" Tucker asked.

She smiled and said, "He does his best. So, is there any news, Mallory?"

"No," she replied. "Which is why we're here. I was hoping we could have a word?"

"Um, sure. Of course." Sarah looked back at the others on the field. "I'm almost done with my afternoon practice. If you'd like to drive over to the oak trees over there beside the barn," she said, turning in the saddle and pointing to the trees, "there are a couple of tables and some benches. I'll take him in and meet you there."

"Fine," Mallory said. "See you in a minute, then."

Sarah nodded, wheeled the big horse around, touched him with her heels and cantered back to where the small group of spectators was waiting for her.

"So, these people are nice, are they?" Tucker asked.

"Of course," Mallory replied. "Why wouldn't they be?"

"I dunno," Tucker said. "I've run into people like these before, and I can't say it was ever a rewarding experience."

"What do you mean, 'people like these'?" she asked, frowning. "They're nice. I've known Sarah since she was in kindergarten."

CHAPTER 18

"Oh... nothing." Tucker shook his head. "It's just that... Oh forget it. I was just trying to get your feel for these people, is all. Money, vast amounts of money, so I've found, can change people."

"The Alexanders have always been very nice to me," she said as she parked next to the small stand of oak trees. "Which, if you consider I'm just a barkeep in a clip joint, says a lot, don't you think?"

Tucker sighed. "I think..." Tucker began, then hesitated before continuing. "I think you tend to put yourself down. I also think you think you know someone, but you really don't. You never really know anyone."

"That's... a horrible outlook to have," she replied, twisting in her seat to look at him. "What you're really saying is that you don't trust *anyone*."

He shrugged. "That's not... exactly true, but in this case, you say you've known Sarah since she was a child, that she's Julie's best friend. But here we are. Julie's missing, and she was perhaps the last person to see her, and she's never bothered to tell you? Why not? Does she know something? Is she hiding something?"

"Let's find out, shall we?" Mallory said, opening the car door and sliding out.

Tucker smiled grimly and did the same. During his years as an FBI agent and, lately, a PI, he'd met a long list of so-called "nice" wealthy people.

Oh, he was just the nicest boy...

She was always so quiet...

And one in particular, *He wouldn't hurt a fly. Why I've seen him rescue bugs from the pool.*

That one murdered two teenage hookers. It was only down to luck that they caught him before he murdered a third.

And now, he thought, *but they were best friends. Geez.*

19

SATURDAY AFTERNOON 2 PM

Mallory could hardly believe he'd said that. *You never really know anyone? What's that about, for Pete's sake? I barely know you, Tucker...* But before she could finish the thought—

"Hey, you two," Sarah said as she joined them and sat down at the picnic table opposite them. "Nellie, my groom, is currying Buckeye for me, so I have a few minutes. What did you want to talk about?"

Tucker opened his mouth to speak. His intention was to put her at ease, but before he could, Mallory jumped in.

"Sarah," she said, staring her in the eyes, "we know you were with Julie just before she disappeared that morning. Why didn't you tell me?"

Whatever Sarah had been expecting Mallory to say, that clearly wasn't it.

"*What?* What are you saying, Mallory?" she snapped. "Are you implying that I had something to do with it? If you are, you're crazy."

"I'm not accusing you of anything," Mallory snapped

back. "But you were there that morning. You should have said something. Why wouldn't you, knowing she was missing?"

"I did," she said, now on the defensive. "I told the sheriff, and I told Kal Cundiff, and he acted like it was no big deal. I told him that Julie and I arranged to meet at the trailhead at seven. We usually drove up there together, but I told him we took two cars because I had to get back to meet my dad at the vet at noon, and that we hiked back to the trailhead together. I left her there at a little after eleven. What she did after I left, I have no idea. She certainly didn't tell me, and when I told Kal about it, he said something like, 'It doesn't matter who she was with at eight if she disappeared at twelve' or something like that. And now you come here accusing me... I can't believe you'd do that, Mallory. I mean... We're friends."

Mallory glanced at Tucker. He was taking notes.

"She took you to meet Zach Burns that morning, didn't she?" Mallory asked. "So what was the big secret? Why did she want you to meet him?"

Tucker looked at Sarah. The question had obviously made her uncomfortable.

She knows something, he thought, watching her struggle to come up with an answer.

"Well, she didn't exactly tell me," Sarah said, "but I figured it out. She was waiting for me at the trailhead—"

"Which one?" Mallory asked.

Sarah frowned. "Does it matter?" she said. "Red Grove East. Anyway," she continued, "before we started out on the hike that morning, she said she had something she wanted to tell me. But she didn't. And when I told her she'd promised to tell me, she said something like, 'Oh, it was nothing important. Forget it.' Well, whatever. Anyway, I'm pretty sure it was something to do with Kal Cundiff."

"What about Kal Cundiff?" Mallory asked.

"Well, they were dating for a while. You knew that, right?" Sarah said.

Tucker looked at Mallory. She looked stunned.

"Uh, uh... No! You can't be serious," Mallory stuttered.

"Oh, but I am," Sarah replied. "They were on and off for months." She looked at Mallory, then at Tucker, then at Mallory again and said, "She once told me that Kal was up to his britches in crap and wading in deeper. That was around the time she broke it off. But I know Julie, and she's been acting all squirrelly again like she does when she likes a guy. And Kal said he'd been talking to her—that was when I was at the sheriff's department—and he said he hadn't heard from her. I think she was getting ready to tell everyone they were a couple."

"But why didn't she tell any of us?" Mallory demanded.

"Well, Mal, you know..." Sarah hesitated.

"What do I know?"

"I mean, she knows how you listen to all those true crime things on the internet," Sarah said. "And well, Kal... If he really is into something—and from what she told me, he probably is—she wouldn't want to say anything because she figured you'd make a big fuss about it... and Kal."

"I don't believe what I'm hearing," Mallory said, shaking her head. "What the hell could Kal be doing that I would make a fuss... about? Oh no. You're not telling me he's a bent cop, are you?"

Sarah nodded slowly and said, "The rumor is that Kal has ties to the moonshiners."

Mallory stared at her, her mouth hanging open. She gulped, looked at Tucker, then at Sarah. She was speechless. She felt numb, and all she could think of was the words Tucker had spoken a few minutes ago, "You never really know anyone." *What else didn't I know?*

She listened to Tucker ask Sarah questions about their hike that morning and how Julie had wanted her to meet Zach Burns, "a ridiculously big man with a black beard," which she did, but wasn't impressed. She said he smelled like one of her horses, and while she loved that smell, it wasn't something she was looking for in a man, and that Zach could have been Grizzly Adams' twin, "Ugh!"

And for once, during the entire conversation, Mallory couldn't help but agree with her. The thought of being in the arms of such a gorilla of a man made her shudder.

And so Tucker continued to question her for several more minutes, but she, Mallory, at least, learned nothing new. What she did know, however, was that Kal Cundiff knew a lot more than he was telling—shifty little son-of-a —and that if Julie had stumbled onto, or into, something she shouldn't... Well, after listening to all those podcasts, she could come up with only one solution, and it was something she didn't want to even contemplate.

And what good was all that listening? she thought. *Hours and hours, and I have to find out from Sarah fricking Alexander that Kal Cundiff is bent, taking bribes? Why the hell didn't I figure that out? Creepy little... If he—*

The thought was interrupted when Sarah suddenly got up out of the seat, walked around the table, sat down beside her and gave her a big hug.

Mallory was shocked but returned the hug, cheeks together, arms wrapped around each other.

"I'm sorry, Mal," Sarah whispered in her ear. "I mean, if I messed up... I'm so sorry."

"It's okay," Mallory said without feeling and without knowing what else to say. "It's not your fault."

"Thanks," Sarah said. "It... It means a lot to hear you say that." Then she kissed Mallory on the cheek, stood up and walked away without a backward look until she reached the barn, where she stopped, turned and gave them a little wave.

"What a load of grade-A *crap*," Tucker said.

Mallory looked at him. "What? What are you talking about, Tucker? She—"

"No, not her," he said. "The crap the sheriff's office has been feeding me."

"I'm sorry, Tucker," Mallory murmured.

"Don't be," he replied. "It was my choice, but I need to talk to Kal Cundiff now. The problem is, I just can't go barging in there. He'll know something's up. I need to make an appointment..." he said thoughtfully. "I need an excuse. Any ideas?"

"No. None. Why don't you let me talk to him? I'll give him something to think about," she said, then added, "Oh dear. Oh—"

"Mallory? Are you all right?"

She blinked, nodded and said, "Yes... I just—"

"Here, give me your keys," he said. "I'll drive you home, okay?"

The thought of "never-clutched" Tucker Randall tearing up her gearbox was just enough to snap Mallory out of whatever fugue she'd been in. She laughed and said, "In your dreams, big fellah. I'm not going to sit there and listen to you grinding my gears all the way home. Get in. I'm all right. I promise."

Despite his dour look and her unsettled stomach, she managed a tiny smile at his obvious discomfort at the idea of her taking the wheel again, especially after the wild ride from Zach Burns' cabin.

The drive home was... silent, at least as far as Mallory was concerned, which was more than a little uncharacteristic. Tucker, however, more than made up for her lack of conversation: making comments about Kal Cundiff, how to make an appointment without tipping him off, and even about the big black horse.

Ten minutes out from her home, she looked at him and said wearily, "You can come in if you like. I'll make some coffee. I just need a few minutes to get ready."

"Get ready? Get ready for what?" he asked.

"For work, of course," she replied. "I have to be at work by five o'clock. It's almost four now. So I can drop you off at your car before I go to work."

"What are you talking about, Mallory? My car's at your place, remember? Are you sure you're all right?" he asked.

"Oh, yeah. Right… You came to my place this morning, didn't you? Yes, of course I am. I'm fine."

Ten minutes later, she parked her truck in the driveway next to Tucker's SUV, mounted the steps to the front door, unlocked it, stepped inside and tripped over an ecstatic Annie and suddenly found herself on her knees on the carpet.

"It's okay," she said as Tucker rushed to her side. "I'm fine. I… Oh, come on, Tucker. I said I'm fine," she said as he helped her to her feet.

"I know you are," he said skeptically, "but why don't you sit down on the couch for a minute and get your breath back?"

"I have to let Annie out."

"I can do that," he said. "You sit still for a minute and take it easy. You've had a rough two weeks. I'll make the coffee."

He stood back and looked down at her. She looked pathetic, staring up at him.

"Stay there," he repeated. "Come on, Annie."

CHAPTER 19

It was almost ten o'clock when Mallory woke up with a start from her nightmare. Not just any nightmare; *the* nightmare, the one she'd been having ever since Julie had disappeared. *What happened?* she thought as she fumbled around in the dark. *Why is it so dark? Where am I? Oh, my God. What time is it? I'm supposed to be at work.*

But she was on top of her bed, still in her hiking clothes. She swung her legs off the bed and sat up, feeling gritty and grungy, and badly in need of a shower.

The phone in her pocket buzzed. She took it out and looked at it. It was just a missed call from an unfamiliar number. "Probably spam," she muttered as she noted the time. It was five after ten. "Geez. Vinnie will be furious. He'll fire me for sure."

She made her way slowly downstairs and found Tucker and Annie sleeping soundly together on the couch.

Now when we came home, he told me to sit on the couch, so how come I was on the bed and he's on the couch? Geez, he must have carried me upstairs. Who does that?

"Hey, macho man," she said, shaking him awake. "What the hell happened? I'm supposed to be at work, and you're supposed to be at home."

He looked up at her and said, "You know, you need to turn the heat up. You could hang meat in here."

"I like to sleep in the cold," she replied. "I'm hungry. I need food. Do you need food?"

"Yes, I could eat something," he said, pushing Annie to one side—who rolled onto her back and stuck all four legs in the air—and he sat up and rubbed his eyes. "You were out of it," he said, "so I thought I'd stay for a while, just in case."

"In case of what?" she asked, looking down at him, smiling, her hands on her hips,

"I dunno," he snapped. "Just in case, okay? What've you got to eat?"

"I'll find something," she said, "but first I need to call Vinnie and apologize for not turning up. It will probably be the end of my illustrious career as head barkeep and bottle washer."

"He already called," Tucker said. "I told him you were exhausted and had gone to bed. To say he wasn't pleased… Well, you may be right."

Shit! she thought. *I really need my job. Oh well, I'll just have to schmooze him a little. In the meantime…*

"Come on," she said. "Let's go to the kitchen. I'll put the heat up a little, pansy boy."

She adjusted the thermostat up two degrees and then went to the refrigerator. "It won't be much, I'm afraid," she said, looking at the remains of a three-day-old Chinese takeout, a half-empty quart of milk, and four eggs. "I need to go grocery shopping. Pancakes be okay?"

"Pancakes? At eleven o'clock at night? Sure, that sounds good. Anything I can do?"

"No. They'll only take a minute," she replied.

"I can't remember the last time someone cooked pancakes for me," Tucker said some five minutes later as she set a short stack down in front of him. "Well, except for IHOP, that is."

"I hope you like them," she said. "I don't do cooking anymore. When Mom got sick, I had to take over the cooking for the family. I'm not good at it, and I hated it. When Mom and then Dad passed, I basically quit."

For several moments they ate in silence, then Tucker said, "By the way, I made an appointment to see Kal Cundiff tomorrow."

"That's good," she replied. "You want me to come with you?"

He shook his head. "No. If he has history with Julie, he'll not be too inclined to talk in front of you."

She looked at him and frowned. "I suppose…" she said, seemingly unconvinced.

"It'll be okay," Tucker said. "What d'you know about his father?"

"Not much. Only that Kevin Cundiff is a gnarled old oak," Mallory said, slowly shaking her head. "He won't bend, Tucker, and I don't think Kal will talk to you. He might talk to me though."

Again, Tucker shook his head. "He'll talk. I'll make him. It's what I do, remember? I was thinking they—the police—were just negligent, but now…" He paused and shook his head, staring down at what was left of his pancakes, then looked up at her and said, "No, I don't think they were negligent. I think their reluctance to investigate Julie's disappearance was a deliberate attempt to cover up whatever it is they're doing. And we need to find out what that is."

"But you don't think Kal could have had something to do with Julie's disappearance, do you?" Mallory asked.

"I don't know," Tucker replied. "I've known a lot of crooked cops, and in my experience, a bad cop is capable of just about anything."

"Yes, but Kal? I've known him forever."

"Yes, well," he said, "you think you know someone, but—"

"—but you really don't," Mallory interrupted and finished for him. "I know, I know, but I still can't believe Kal would hurt Julie."

"Yes, well," he repeated, pushing his empty plate away. "We've had a tough couple of weeks and it's getting late. I need to go home and get some sleep, and so do you."

"Yes," she said halfheartedly. "But you could stay here if you like… on the couch."

Tucker smiled at her and said, "Thanks, but that wouldn't be a good idea, now would it? What would the neighbors say? And besides, if I stay here, I'll still have to go home in the morning. So, I'll bid you goodnight and see you tomorrow after I've talked to the deputy?"

"Umm, yes, I guess," she said.

He nodded, stood up and said, "Get some sleep, Mallory. And try not to worry about things you can't change."

She rose to her feet and walked him to the door.

"Thanks for all you do, Tucker," she said as he opened the door. "I really do appreciate it."

"My pleasure," he said and winked at her. Then he walked quickly down the steps to his car and drove away into the night, leaving her standing just inside the open door staring after him.

20

SUNDAY MORNING 10AM

It was getting on for ten o'clock that Sunday morning when Tucker parked in a visitor's spot outside the sheriff's office.

He sat for a moment staring at the glass front entrance, getting his thoughts together. This was not, he knew, going to be a friendly meeting; more of a confrontation.

Finally, he took a deep breath and exited the vehicle. The perky desk sergeant he was used to dealing with was nowhere to be seen, but Sheriff Cundiff was.

"He's not here," Cundiff said when Tucker asked to see the deputy. "What d'you want him for?"

"I have an appointment with him at ten," Tucker replied, looking at his watch. "It's almost ten now. Where is he?"

"I told you. He's not here. He has a scheduled patrol this morning," Cundiff explained. "You sure you got the right day? It is Sunday, you know?"

"Yes, I have the right day. I talked to him at around seven yesterday evening. He said ten o'clock, and here I am."

"Well, Randall, you drove all this way for nothing, didn't you?" he said and began to turn away.

"I don't think so, Sheriff," Tucker said easily. "What I need to talk to him about is important, so why don't you get on the radio and have him come on in?"

Cundiff turned to face him again, a look of disdain on his face.

"You're not a Fed anymore, Randall. You can't..." he began, then caught the look on Tucker's face and changed his mind. "Ah, what the hell," he continued, "but it better be important."

He keyed his radio and said, "You forget your appointment this morning, boy? Get your ass in here now."

Less than fifteen minutes later, Kal Cundiff, looking flustered and more than a little wary, walked into the department and looked around.

"Good morning, Deputy," Tucker said, stepping up behind him. "I thought we had an appointment?"

"Yeah. I forgot. Sorry. What d'you want to talk to me about?"

"You want to do this out here, in the lobby, where everyone can hear?" Tucker asked quietly.

Cundiff frowned, looked around at the several deputies who were chatting together, then muttered something Tucker couldn't hear. He assumed it wasn't a compliment.

"This way," Kal said, pushing open the door to a small conference room. "We can talk in here."

Tucker nodded and stepped inside, then turned to look at the deputy.

"Siddown, why don't ya?" Kal Cundiff said, glaring at him.

CHAPTER 20

Tucker smiled, shook his head, sat down at the table, and said, "Who kicked your cat this morning, Kal?"

Cundiff sat down opposite him, leaned on the table, narrowed his eyes, and said, "What's this all about, Randall? You're about to get me into trouble, havin' the sheriff drag me in off patrol like you did. What is it you want? Spit it out. I ain't got all day."

"I'm here to talk to you about Julie Romero," Tucker said. "Any comment?"

"Comment?" he said. "Why would I have any comment? No, I don't have no comment."

"You didn't talk to her that day she went missing?" Tucker asked. "Think about it, Kal. It was a Wednesday."

"No. I didn't."

"That's not quite true, is it, Kal?" Tucker asked.

"What're you trying to say, dickhead? That I had somethin' to do with Julie's disappearance? Well I didn't, see? So you can quit barking up that tree."

"I didn't say you did," Tucker said quietly. "I was just wondering if you spoke to her, that's all."

"Didn't say a word to her," Cundiff snapped. "We done here?" He started to get up.

"No, we're not done here, Kal. Far from it. Sit down. You say you didn't talk to her?" He stared Cundiff in the eye and inwardly smiled when he saw his eyes flicker and look away to the left.

"That's what I said," he replied.

"So, if I were to look through the impressive stack of text messages Mallory downloaded from Julie's phone, I wouldn't find anything there?"

Kal frowned, looked away, just for a second, then stared at Tucker and said, "I don't text Julie's phone." And Tucker, for once, didn't think the deputy was lying. But there was something else there; he wasn't lying, but…

I don't text Julie's phone! Hmm. So, if he wasn't lying, does that mean he texts to something else, a computer, maybe?

"But you were seeing her, weren't you?" Tucker said.

"What? No, well not—" He was angry. "Oh, I get it. You're trying to pin it on me. Well it won't work. Yeah, I was seeing her; nothin' serious. We just dated a little, back a few months ago. But she broke up with me. Who you bin talkin' to, Randall? I bet it was that stuck-up little heifer, Sarah Alexander. Sneaky little cow, she is. I never could understand why Julie hung around that little gossip."

"I haven't spoken to her," Tucker lied. "I just listened to what people were saying. It wasn't much of a secret, was it? And, from what I was able to piece together, it seems you two have ... let's say, some unresolved issues?"

"Bullcrap," Cundiff snapped.

Tucker nodded and smiled at him. "No problem. I know a guy who does excellent work on phones... and computers," Tucker said. "I'll just hand her devices over to him and see what he comes up with. But... you need to know, my friend, if I find anything of yours, you're going to have some serious explaining to do." And with that, Tucker stood up and turned toward the door.

"All right! All right," Kal said and swore loudly. "Sit down, damn it. Okay, so we... we use an app. It's supposed to be for discreet chats. It's called Significant, or Syllable, or something like that. I know it begins with an S. Even after she broke up with me, she'd talk to me sometimes. I always thought..." His forehead wrinkled. His eyes closed to mere slits. "I always thought we'd get back together, but then she told me she was seeing someone else."

Now it was Tucker's turn to frown. "You sure? Did she say who it was?" he asked.

Cundiff shook his head. "Yeah, I'm sure. She flat-out told me. No, she never said who it was."

CHAPTER 20

"But do *you* know who it is?"

Cundiff looked at him and said, "No... I don't."

Tucker nodded and changed direction. "Where were you that morning, Kal? Tell me, and if it checks out, I'll go look somewhere else."

Kal froze, his eyes wide. "Hey. I'm a frickin' deputy," he said. "You're not a cop anymore, so I don't have to tell you nothin'."

Tucker nodded, stood up again, walked to the door, then turned and said, "That's right, Kal. You don't. But if you have nothing to hide, you'd talk to me, which leads me to believe two things. One, you do have something to hide, and I'm pretty sure I know what that is. And two, you don't have an alibi for that morning, and you know what happened to her. I think it's time we brought the state police into this." He turned again and pulled the door open.

Kal leapt out of his chair, charged around the table, shoved the door shut with a bang, and stood with his nose almost touching Tucker's, his face twisted with rage.

"You jumped-up son of a bitch," he shouted. "What the hell d'you think you're doin'?"

"I'm doing my job, Kal," Tucker replied quietly. "While you seem to be a disgrace to yours."

Kal drew back his fist, just as Tucker had expected.

Too slow, he thought as Kal swung at his face. He leaned a little to his right. The punch slid by. Tucker grabbed his wrist, snapped it behind his back, and slammed the deputy face-first against the wall.

"Tut, tut," he whispered in Kal's ear. "One of the first things the FBI teaches new recruits is how to dodge a lousy punch," he whispered as he increased the pressure, and Kal's heels lifted off the floor.

"Now stop embarrassing yourself and your father,"

Tucker said, "and tell me where you were so I can move on."

Kal struggled in his grip, puffed for breath, then yelped, "Okay, okay. Lemme go," he gasped. "I'll tell ya."

Tucker released him and Kal stumbled forward, then turned to face him, his face red, his teeth bared, his hand on his weapon.

"You're going to shoot me here, knowing I'm unarmed? How d'you think that will go down, Kal?" Tucker taunted him. "Even your daddy couldn't get you out of that one."

Kal's face twisted with rage, but his hand dropped away from his gun.

"Look," he said, "the Cundiffs have been here since we moved from Virginia back in the seventeen fifties. We know these mountains, the forest and the trails, and we used them to move... trade goods. We smuggled supplies past the British, and we stole Union gold and delivered it to Jefferson Davis. In the thirties, we moved shine, and then weed startin' in the fifties. It's what we do; always have done. People still pay well for good moonshine, and ours is the best."

"Marijuana, you say?" Tucker asked. "It's legal in most states now."

Cundiff scoffed. "Hahaha. Yeah, that regulated medicinal crap. But anything worth smoking has to be farmed proper, like. Not that I do that," he added quickly. "Our main still is not far from the trail that Julie liked to walk. It's on Cundiff land, not that anyone notices, or even cares."

"You still haven't answered my question," Tucker said. "Where were you between eleven and five the afternoon she disappeared?"

"I was on the other side of the county, almost to Etowah, taking care of official business. We had a problem

CHAPTER 20

with one of our, um, transports. You can check the duty logs on that. And I already told everyone in the family that she was off limits and they was to leave her alone. If someone in the family had done something to her, I'd've been told."

Maybe you'd like to think that, Tucker thought, watching Cundiff stare belligerently at him. *But I'm not sure you think at all.*

"So, are we good now?" Cundiff asked. "Cause if we are, and you're done askin' your questions, you can kindly shove off and let me get on with my day." His eyes narrowed. The corners of his lips turned upward to form what might have been a humorless smile. "Or maybe I should ask a few of my family members to pay you a visit. You don't wanna meet them, I promise."

"Kal," Tucker said, "you're about as smart as a one-eyed donkey. That camera up there behind you has been on the whole time we've been talking."

He spun around, looked up at the camera and was about to speak when the door opened and two deputies rushed in.

"You okay, Kal?" one of them said, his hand on his gun.

"Yeah. I'm good," he snapped. "*Mr.* Randall was just leaving. See him out, will you?"

Well now, that was interesting, Tucker thought as he made his way down the steps to his car. *That was quite an information dump he dropped in my lap.*

Tucker fished the micro recorder from his pocket and turned it off, grinning to himself. *Not that it would be admissible, but it certainly would be useful to an outside investigator.*

Five minutes later he was on sixty-four heading back toward Chattanooga, singing along with George Jones on Willie's Roadhouse. "He stopped loving her today…"

Tucker was on I-75 heading south past the Ooltewah exit when he called Mallory.

"Tucker," she said. "What's up?"

"Here's a silly question," he replied. "Does Julie have a computer?"

"Yes, of course. Who doesn't? Why d'you ask?"

"She and Kal Cundiff have been communicating through some kind of secret app. I want to know what they've been talking about. Where is it?"

"It's at Jennifer's. We could take a look at it."

"Has anyone else looked at it? The law, for instance?"

"Well, yes. Kal stopped by and looked at it. He said there's nothing on it."

Of course he did. He would, wouldn't he?

"When did he look at it?" he asked.

"I don't know, not for sure. More than a week ago. I guess we could find out."

"I'm on my way back now. I'll pick you up in say… ten minutes? We'll grab a quick sandwich and then go see what we can see."

"I have to be at work at five," she said. "That gives me at least a couple of hours. I can't be late, though. I missed work yesterday. I can't understand why Vinnie hasn't called me."

"Mallory, I told you. He called last night," Tucker said.

"Yeah," she said. "I remember. I also remember I said I was going to give him a piece of my mind when I get there tonight. Still, I thought he would have called today. He'd need to know if he needed to get someone to cover for me."

"You don't have to go, you know."

"Oh, you don't think I'm gonna pass up the opportunity

to gut the little creep like a fish, do you?" He thought he could hear her teeth grinding. "But we have a couple hours yet. What dirt did you manage to dig up on Kal?"

"You can listen to it on the way to Jennifer's. I'll be there in just a few minutes."

21

SUNDAY AFTERNOON 2PM

It was a little after two o'clock when they arrived at the Romero home. Jennifer opened the front door, her eyes red and swollen. "Oh. Hi, Mallory," she said before catching a glimpse of Tucker behind her. "Oh, and you, Mr. Randall! Do you have any news for us?"

Before he could answer, however, Mallory said, "Jen, I tried to call you three times to tell you we were on the way, but your phone went straight to voice mail. Have you turned it off? Is everything okay? You don't look well."

"I'm fine," she said, taking the phone from her pocket. "I'm just tired, is all. Oh dear. It's dead. I guess I forgot to charge it again. I can't seem to remember anything these days." She put the phone back in her pocket. "You'd better come in. You have news, right?"

"Nothing new. Sorry," Mallory replied as they followed her into the kitchen. "But we do need to look at Julie's computer, Jen. Is that okay?"

"Why d'you need to do that?" Jen asked. "The police already looked at it."

"Kal Cundiff, right?" Mallory asked.

Jen nodded.

"That's why we need to look at it," Mallory said dryly. "In her bedroom?"

"Yes, but what did you mean about Kal? He's a deputy."

"It's a long story," Tucker said. "And we need to confirm it."

"Of course, of course," Jennifer said. "Upstairs, second on the... Why am I telling you, Mal? You know where it is. Go on up. I'll be down here if you need me."

Mallory paused outside Julie's bedroom door, looked at Tucker, nodded and pushed the door open.

The room was neat and tidy, the bed made, the dresser and bedside table tops neatly ordered, and the few papers and notebooks on the small desk under the window arranged neatly around a MacBook Air laptop.

"I don't even want to be in here," Mallory said. "Too many memories. Painting each other's nails, watching the silly shows on her little TV, and helping her choose photos to make collages next to the mirror. Hmm, the mirror's been moved, and the pictures are different. The little TV's been replaced by a flatscreen. The bookcase is new. So is the Xbox. When did she start playing that, I wonder?"

She stood for a moment while Tucker went to the laptop.

Wow, how little I know her since she's grown up, Mallory thought as she looked at the photographs.

"It's still plugged in," Tucker said as he sat down and lifted the lid and tapped the spacebar. "No password. We're in," he said, looking at the crowded desktop display. "I'm surprised."

"I'm not," she replied. "Julie was always careless about stuff like that. Same with her phone."

"I guess she trusted her mom and dad, then," Tucker said as he scrolled through her files.

"Oh, they wouldn't touch her stuff... Heck, I don't think they'd know how to. If she didn't take it anywhere, she wouldn't see the need." Mallory sighed. "I told her she needs to use a password to keep hackers and malware out, but all she said was, 'why would anyone want to hack little old me?'"

Tucker frowned, barely listening to her. He picked up a small black object from the top of a pile of notebooks. "Hey, see this?" He held it up for her to see. It looked like a cell phone, except instead of a screen, the face was a display of tiny photo cells.

"Looks like a phone," Mallory said. "I didn't know she has two."

"It's not a phone," Tucker said. "It's a solar power cell. You use it for charging cell phones. I saw one just like it on the sideboard in Zach Burns' cabin," he said.

"So Burns has a cell phone, then," Mallory said. "Interesting, but not surprising. Everybody has one. Even mountain men like Zach Burns. I wonder if he has a computer as well?"

"What did Kal say the program was called?" Tucker asked.

"Syllable, I think. Or something like it," she replied.

"There's nothing like that here," Tucker said.

"Let me try," Mallory said.

Tucker pushed the chair back and stood up. Mallory sat down, looked at the screen and said, "You're right. Let's try this." And she clicked the Launchpad icon.

"There," she said. "Look at that. SeaMonkey, Spacejock, Spybot, Stardock, Startup folder... STD? Oh, STDUtility, some kind of PDF viewer. Stellarium, and SUPERAntiSpyware. Nothing."

"Go back to the other screen," Tucker said. "Let's see what we... there." He pointed. "Open that folder, the one labeled TAHC."

Mallory opened the folder and found icons for a dozen more programs. "AOL Instant Messenger?" she asked. "Is she even old enough to know about AOL? Googlechat, MSN chat, Sibilant, Trillian—"

"Sibilant," Tucker said. "Try that one."

Mallory clicked the icon and up popped up a long list of chat histories.

"Clever girl," Tucker said. "TAHC is chat spelled backwards."

"Sneaky, more like," Mallory muttered. "I still think a password would be better... Geez, there are a lot of chats here. I wonder if she uses the same account for her phone too. Can we get her phone records?"

"The sheriff's department should have done that, but they didn't," Tucker said. "I suggested they do so to Sheriff Cundiff, and he said he'd need to get a warrant. Click on the last one. The one dated the thirteenth."

She did and up popped:

DeputyDawg: *09:30*
i was thinking we could go on a hike
tomorrow for old times sake

Makelikeatree: *09:34*
I wish you would stop this, Kal
I told you I'm not interested

DeputyDawg: *09:35*

we had something good before babe
no reason we can't make it work
this other guy don't have what I can offer

Makelikeatree: *09:37*
I'm trying to enjoy time with my friend
If you have to talk, at least wait until after lunch

DeputyDawg: *09:38*
what you out with sarah again
dunno why you hang with her
she's just an airhead

Makelikeatree: *10:03*
Didn't you ever hear the song?
If you wanna be my lover, you gotta get with my friends
Insulting my best friend is a stupid way to convince me that you're interested

DeputyDawg: *10:05*
whats it take for you to say yes again
DeputyDawg: *10:45*
Julie when will you say yes again
DeputyDawg: *11:08*
gotta go out to the county border
someone pulled over the wrong car and now
i gotta deal with it
cant trust anyone

Makelikeatree: *11:55*
I'm about to say yes, Kal
Just not to you

DeputyDawg: *12:24*
who the crap you keep talkin' about
DeputyDawg: *12:39*
come on babe talk to me
DeputyDawg: *12:57*
Julie why you gotta be like this

"Why does she still have this program if all she does is argue with Kal?" Mallory asked. "And who is she seeing?"

"Go back to the list... Yep... Good... Click on that one labeled Ogre."

Mallory clicked, then narrowed her eyes and said, "Ogre? Who the hell is Ogre?"

"There," Tucker said. "Open the last chat marked the eleventh."

AintNoMountain: *19:12*
I'm really looking forward to
introducing you to Sarah
She's been my best friend for years

Ogre: *19:23*
I don't know if this is a good idea
I'm not that kind of guy

AintNoMountain: *19:25*
No, everything is going to be fine.
I promise
Sarah is really nice

Mallory looked at Tucker and said, "Ogre's Zach Burns."

"Yup," Tucker said, smiling.

Ogre: *19:31*
Nice people don't like me.
Whoops. I spelled that wrong. People

AintNoMountain: *19:32*
If they don't like you, then they can't be very nice, can they?

Ogre: *19:40*
Why are you so nice to me, Julie?
Nobody else is
You're an angel
you're

AintNoMountain: *19:42*
I like to be nice to everyone
I'm an angel?
Why did you change your name to Ogre?

Ogre: *19:54*
I feel like an ogre

AintNoMountain: *19:55*
You're not an ogre
You're the sweetest and most gentle man I've ever met
And I'm sure Sarah will think the same

"Well, that didn't happen, did it?" Tucker said. "Sarah said she thought he smelled funny."

But Mallory didn't hear him, or if she did, she didn't reply. She just sat there staring at the screen. *'You are the sweetest and most gentle man I've ever met.'* If she said that, Mallory thought, *she meant it, but then, Julie always thinks the best of everyone.*

Then Tucker's words sank in. "Yes, she said he smelled like one of her horses. Can't say I noticed anything like that, but then, I didn't get that close to him."

"Mallory, this is two days before Sarah went on the hike with Julie," Tucker said. "Ogre is Zach Burns." He tossed the charger in the air and caught it. "I guess our mountain man needs a phone to talk to the ladies."

"Makes sense," Mallory said thoughtfully.

"We need to document everything," Tucker said. "We need to download and print everything."

Mallory looked at the time, then turned to look at him and said, "It's after three. I want to go in to work early. I need to talk to Vinnie, so I need to go home and get ready. I'll ask Jen if I can take the computer with us." She traced the cord to the wall and pulled it free.

It was almost four o'clock when Mallory pushed through the front entrance of The Saloon to a round of wolf whistles from the gathered gentry seated at the bar and in the booths.

She ignored them and walked quickly to the bar where Roger was busy cleaning a glass.

"Roger, *where* is Vinnie?" she asked angrily.

"Last I saw, he was in his office." Roger gave her a strange look. "I don't think you're... He asked me to cover for you tonight. He said he didn't think your new friend would be letting you out."

"Did he now?" Mallory snapped. "Son of a bitch," she muttered as she rounded the end of the bar, pushed past Roger, marched to Vinnie's office door and shoved it open so hard the knob slammed against the wall.

"Vinnie! What the hell have you been telling everybody?" she shouted.

He looked up from counting cash. "Ah. There you are. I figured you'd be takin' another night off, so I asked Roger to fill in for you. Good night last night?" he asked, a nasty little smile on his lips.

"You're an evil little man, you know that?" she yelled. "You know what I've been going through ever since my niece went missing, and you just don't give a damn, do you? Why did you say all those horrible things about me?"

"How could anybody forget?" He shrugged as he laid the handful of bills down. "You never shut up about it."

"You told everyone I was having sex with Tucker Randall last night. Didn't you? I wasn't. I wouldn't. I hardly know him. I was exhausted. I passed out at three in the afternoon after hiking over half the damn mountain."

"And he picked up the phone when I called," Vinnie said. "How'm I supposed to know you weren't—"

"You insensitive little son of a bitch. How dare you make up this kind of garbage?"

"Seemed legit to me," he said, grinning at her. "If he'd done the job right, you wouldn't be in here screaming at me."

She stared at him, unable to believe what she was hearing. "You nasty, nasty little man. You think that? Very well, then, I'll give you something to smile about." And she turned on her heel and walked out.

"Wait!" Vinnie shouted as she pushed past Roger again

and stopped at the "high-end" rack. She turned the spotlights on, took out her phone and took three photos making sure her camera recorded the details of each and every bottle. Then she swept each and every bottle off of the shelves, jumping back as she cleared each shelf and the bottles crashed down onto the floor, shattering, sending an explosion of broken glass and booze almost from one end of the bar to the other, prompting another round of cheering and hooting from the assembled drinkers.

Vinnie finally caught up to her, shook his fist in her face, and yelled, "You're gonna pay for that."

"Sure I will," she retorted. "Bill me," she taunted. "I took pictures of everything you had up there. It was nothing but a collection of nearly empty bottles. If you get five hundred for the entire mess, it'll be too generous."

"You can't do that!" Vinnie insisted. "What kinda person are you?"

"What kind of person tells a room full of people that his 'best bartender'"—she made quotes with her fingers—"is getting laid while she's out looking for a missing family member, you insensitive little shit? And I can guarantee you this, if you even try to get me for the booze, I will hit you for slander, defamation, loss of public standing, and I'll call the Public Health office and tell them exactly what kind of dump you're running here. They'll close you down for good." She turned to leave.

"You know what? You're fired!" Vinnie yelled after her.

"Too late, you gormless little sloth," she shouted over her shoulder. "I already quit. Come on, Tucker. Let's get the hell out of this hell hole."

Tucker, who'd followed her into the bar, had been sitting calmly in one of the booths talking to two of Vinnie's customers and recording their versions of what Vinnie had told them the night before.

CHAPTER 21

"You know that's not going to be admissible in court," she said as they settled into her truck.

"Oh, but it will. They consented to be recorded, and your lawyer can call them as witnesses. Airtight."

"I can't afford a lawyer," she replied, "and besides, I did do a little property damage."

"That you did," Tucker said. "Much to the delight of the patronage. I doubt he'll do anything about it, though."

"Well, if he does, I'll just sue him for the deed to the place, right?" Mallory asked.

Tucker raised an eyebrow. "I think you need to find yourself some courtroom podcasts. Or at least watch some *Law & Order*."

"And why wouldn't I?" she replied lightly. "I'm going to have a whole lot of free time from now on… Okay, so what now, Sherlock?"

"And that makes you Dr. Watson?" he asked, smiling at her.

"I'd rather be Irene Adler," she said with a grin.

"Scandalous," Tucker replied with a smirk.

"Bohemian," Mallory retorted.

But the moment faded along with Mallory's adrenaline when the gravity of what she'd done began to sink in: she was out of a job with no prospects, and Julie was still missing.

"Hmm," Tucker said. "I think the next step will be to take a deeper look at Zach Burns. After all, if the rumors about him are true, the man's an unconvicted killer, and he obviously knew and was friendly with Julie. If he… and she…" He didn't finish either sentence. Instead, he continued his thought, "I'll pay another visit to the sheriff's office and see if they'll let me take a look at his file."

"I can give you a summary," Mallory said. "His mother died. She was brutally murdered. They never found her body or the murder weapon, but they did find a lot of blood. The DNA test established it was hers. There was so much she couldn't possibly have survived. It's kind of what got me interested in true crime. They found Zach in the house, semi-comatose, with her blood on his clothes. And he claims he remembered nothing, not what happened, how the blood got there, nothing. He was arrested on suspicion of murder, but they had to let him go due to lack of evidence. And then he just disappeared into the wilderness."

"Thanks for that," Tucker said. "It'll help me get through the file faster."

"No problem."

"Well, it's only… four-fifteen," Tucker said, looking at his watch. "How about you take me back to your place to get my car and I leave the laptop with you? You can go through those messages, download and print them while I head over to the sheriff's office and see if I can get a peek at Zach's files."

"Sounds like teamwork," she said. "Glad to be on the team."

He gave her a smile. "Yeah, me too," he said dryly.

22

SUNDAY AFTERNOON, 4:40PM

For the second time that day, Tucker walked briskly into the sheriff's department lobby, confident that, with it being Sunday, both the Cundiffs would be long gone.

"Something I can do for you, Randall?" Sheriff Cundiff said from behind the front desk.

"Er… Yes. That is…" For a moment Tucker was lost for words. *What the hell's he doing here? And why's he at the front desk.*

The sheriff glared at him, his eyes narrowed.

"Well? Come on. Out with it. I don't got all night. Why are you back here again for the second time today?"

"I came to talk to you about Zach Burns. D'you have a minute?"

At first, Cundiff looked surprised, then pleased. "Ah-ha! So, you found our very own 'Boy Who Lived,' complete with scar. Why d'you want to dig up that seedy part of our past?"

Tucker frowned. The sheriff's reaction wasn't quite what he'd expected.

"Just curious," Tucker said cautiously. "He has quite a reputation, and I seem to have run out of leads. If he's a killer, he could at least be a person of interest."

"Well now, I haven't seen that boy in years," Cundiff replied. "Lives somewhere up there in the forest, so they say." He paused, looked at Tucker and, not receiving a reply, he nodded and continued. "Sure, you can look at the file. There's not much to it, though. Come on around this side and watch the desk in case someone comes in, and I'll go get it. Might take a minute, though."

Now there's a surprise, Tucker thought as he watched the sheriff walk away. *Why's he being so cooperative? He must be up to something, but what?*

Then he remembered the younger Cundiff's parting words: "Maybe I should ask a few of my family members to pay you a visit. You don't wanna meet them."

"I guess you were surprised to see me here," Cundiff said as he returned and placed a box on the desk in front of Tucker.

Tucker looked at the box, then at the sheriff, but didn't reply.

"Well, I had paperwork to do," Cundiff continued, "so I sent everyone home." He smiled a strange smile as if he knew something Tucker didn't. But all Tucker said was "Thanks," then opened the box and took out the first folder, flipped it open and glanced at the first page.

"Geez," he said when he turned to the second page, an eight-by-ten photograph of a young boy, his entire midsection covered in blood. His hands and face all had copious amounts of blood on them. "This is Zach Burns?" he asked, looking up at the sheriff.

"Yup! That's him. That was taken the day Wynona

Burns died in her home, alone with her 'little boy.'" Cundiff made quotes with his fingers.

Tucker looked again at the photo of a much younger Zach Burns than the one he'd met in the cabin. He was a tall, heavy-set, clean-shaven man and, but for the blood, a good-looking young man. *What the hell is wrong with this picture?* he thought.

He looked up at the sheriff. He was smiling.

"Hmm," Tucker said. "So, either Zach Burns killed his mother or he knows who did."

"That's about the size of it," Cundiff replied with a smirk. "See, he was found sitting there, in the house, totally out of it; semi-comatose was how the doctor described it." He tilted his head to one side, narrowed his eyes and continued, "He told the detectives, when we finally got him to talk, that he didn't remember anything. He had a nasty wound to the side of his head and a concussion, and he was covered in Wynona Burns' blood, along with some of his own, as you can see." He nodded at the photograph still in Tucker's hand.

"It would have been a slam dunk," Cundiff continued, "except there was no body and no weapon. Oh, we detained him, held him for forty-eight hours, questioned him, but we got no more out of him than he couldn't remember anything." He stared Tucker in the eye for a moment, then said, "We had to let him go, but we haven't closed the books on Wynona's murder, not yet."

"And there was nothing at the crime scene to—"

"No," the sheriff snapped, interrupting him. "Other than Wynona's blood, the place was clean: no prints, other than hers and the boy's, nothing. As I said, had it not been for the absence of the body and the murder weapon, that boy would be in jail to this day."

"So, from what you're telling, it's clear he didn't hack

his mother to death?" Tucker asked. "Because if he did, he must have somehow gotten rid of the body and the weapon, then come back all covered in blood and waited for someone to find him. That makes no sense, Sheriff."

"You think?" Cundiff asked, smiling. "He could have done just that. Let me tell you something, Randall. By the time that boy was twelve, he was as tall as me. He was sixteen years old when his mother died. And, like you, nobody thought he could have done it. But as he got older, he started gettin' a little rough with people. And when he threw a punch at his football coach, people started wondering; if a big, strong fella like Zach Burns could throw a punch at his coach, maybe he did kill his momma.

"Wynona was a slip of a woman; couldn't have weighed more than a hundred-ten. When she died, the boy was six foot tall and was playing linebacker. It would've been a cinch for him to do just as you said: haul her body out of there, dump it in the truck bed and then haul it off somewhere."

"You checked his truck, right?" Tucker asked and immediately regretted it.

"What d'you think we are out here, Randall?" the sheriff snapped. "Of course we checked the damn truck. It was clean."

"He could have wrapped her in a tarp... Okay, okay. I get it. What little you have is circumstantial," Tucker said. "You have no body and no murder weapon. Sure, he took a blow to his head, but it's more likely he could have gotten that trying to protect her rather than fighting with her. And if he did kill her, where did he take the body?"

Cundiff shrugged. "As I said, he was a big fella, even then. I mean really big. He could have carried her off and buried her somewhere. He knows the forest better than anyone."

CHAPTER 22

"Better than you, Sheriff?"

Again the sheriff shrugged, but he said nothing.

"So," Tucker said, "what you're saying is that Burns fought with his mother, killed her, carried her body off into the forest, buried her, *then calmly walked back to the house* and sat down and waited for your people to come and arrest him. I don't buy it."

"Like I said; he's a big fella," Cundiff said for the third time. "And he had a head injury. He could have done it and buried the knife along with her."

"Cadaver dogs?" Tucker asked, already knowing the answer.

"Of course, but have you any idea at all of just how big the forest is? It's more than seven-hundred-thousand acres big. That's how big it is, and as I said, he knows it better than anyone."

Tucker heaved a sigh and shook his head.

Cundiff looked at him and said dryly, "Yeah, right. That's exactly how we all felt. Still do." He paused and then continued, "They sent him off to Memorial for his head, and they treated him. I don't have those records, though. But I likely couldn't show 'em to you anyway, on account of HIPPO."

"You mean HIPAA?" Tucker said dryly as he opened the medical report. "Ah-ha, here's a psych evaluation—"

He saw little more than the name "Dr. John Wilson" before Sheriff Cundiff snatched it away.

"Oops. Forgot that was in there. Yep, HIPAA. Can't be lettin' you see that."

"And you have no other suspects, persons of interest?" Tucker asked, looking the sheriff right in the eye.

Cundiff didn't flinch. He stared right back, then said, slowly, "No. No, sir. Not a one. The Wynona Burns case is cold as the grave, in more ways than one. Now, if we're done. I've got paperwork I need to finish."

Tucker could tell from the look on Cundiff's face that he was through talking; that he'd gotten all he was going to get. So he returned the file to the box, stood up and said, "Thank you, Sheriff. You've been most helpful."

"Glad to be of service, son. You be safe out there. You heah? Oh, and by the way, Kal told me how you ran him around the block earlier today, so let me make this clear, Randall. You keep your nose out of our business. You have no idea what you're messing with."

"I have no interest in your illegal operation, Sheriff," Tucker said. "All I'm interested in is finding Julie Romero, and I think you know more about that than you're willing to let on. I also think you slow-walked the case because it might have interfered with the family business. But that is what it is, and if anyone decides to come after you, it will be because of your own negligence or malfeasance. All I want to do is find the girl."

"You arrogant, know-it-all son of a bitch. Get the hell out of my department, and don't come back. When you find that girl, she's gonna be dead. That's what happens to careless people around here."

"That sounds almost like a threat, Sheriff," Tucker said as he shoved the box back across the desk at him, "or an admission. So! If I were you, I'd try to remember that the least said, the better."

And then, showing far more boldness and confidence than he felt, he walked around the massive desk and strode out the front door.

Well now, that went well, he thought as he opened his car door and slid in behind the wheel. *Smart Tucker wouldn't have riled up a bootlegging sheriff like that. Smart Tucker would have schmoozed him instead.*

But he had learned something new. That quick glimpse of the ME's report had triggered a thought—and a new question.

Why would a GP be doing a psych evaluation on what possibly could have been a mentally deranged teenage boy? It makes no sense... No sense at all.

23

SUNDAY EVENING 5:30PM

On a whim, and for no good reason he could think of, Tucker decided to drive by Dr. Wilson's office. Not that he expected anybody to be there; it was, after all, almost five-thirty on a Sunday evening, and if you were to ask him why he did it, he probably wouldn't be able to tell you, other than it was indeed, just... a whim.

So, it was no little surprise to see not one but two cars parked outside the front entrance to the doctor's office: an expensive Cadillac SUV and an inexpensive, aging Honda Civic.

He parked next to the Civic, noting that the lights were on inside the clinic, and then sat there for a moment wondering if he should go and knock on the door.

"Nothing ventured..." he muttered as he pushed open the car door, stepped out and walked quickly to the entrance. The sign on the inside told him, "Open 8AM to 6PM Mon-Fri. 8AM to 12PM Sat. Closed Sunday."

"Strange." He glanced back at the two vehicles, frowned and then he smiled. "Methinks the good doctor is entertaining."

He looked at his watch. It was five-thirty-five. He raised his hand to knock on the door... then changed his mind, grabbed the handle and pushed and, low and behold, the door opened and he stepped inside.

"Excuse me," a voice said from behind the sliding glass window. "You can't come in here. It's Sunday. We're closed. You need to leave so I can lock the door. We open at eight—"

"I apologize for the intrusion," Tucker said, smiling, "but I saw the cars outside. I was here a couple of days ago, and this..." He pulled back his sleeve enough to show her the bandage. "And I just wanted to ask the good doctor a few questions."

"But we're closed."

"And I only need a few minutes of his time," Tucker insisted with an edge to his voice.

The receptionist looked confused. She obviously didn't know what to do. Tucker looked at her and smiled, and raised his eyebrows in question, then waited for her to speak.

"Very well," she said, picking up the phone. "He's doing... his paperwork. I'll let him know you're here, but he won't be pleased, I can assure you."

She tapped a button, listened for a minute until the doctor picked up, then said, "Doctor Wilson, there's a man here demanding to speak to you. I told him we were closed, but he's insisting. Can you come up here, please? What? Call the p..." She glanced up at Tucker and then whispered into the phone, "No! Absolutely not. You know I can't do that. You come up here and deal with him yourself." And she hung up.

CHAPTER 23

Tucker stepped closer to the window and looked down at her desk. There was a small makeup kit—open—and a name badge. It was facing away from him, but he had no trouble reading it upside down. "Linda Warner."

Linda Warner, if that's who she was, glared at him, stood up, flounced out of the office and disappeared into the depths of the dragon's lair, leaving Tucker smiling hugely in the waiting room.

"Naughty, naughty," he muttered, smiling to himself.

She came back a few moments later, followed by Dr. Wilson.

"Mr. Randall," he said, frowning. "Linda tells me you're having problems with your stitches. Couldn't it have waited until tomorrow morning? I'm in the middle of paperwork... Well, never mind. You're here now, so let's take a look at it, shall we?"

"The stitches are fine—"

"But Linda said—" the doctor interrupted him.

"Yes, I know," Tucker said, interrupting the doctor. "The truth is, I was passing by and I saw your cars parked outside, and I thought perhaps you might take a moment to answer a few questions about the case I'm working on. I mentioned it while you were stitching me up. I'm looking into the disappearance of Julie Romero?"

Wilson stared at him, narrowed his eyes, frowned, then smiled and said, "Of course. Mallory Carver's niece. But... I don't see how I can help. Julie's a patient here, but I've seen her only... well, no more than once a year for the past..." He glanced at Linda through the glass. She was staring at him. "...four years?"

He raised his eyebrows in question. She tapped rapidly on her computer, then nodded and said, "Yes, four years."

"So," he said, looking again at Tucker. "As I said, I hardly know the lady, and I certainly can't reveal any of her medical information. That would be a violation of HIPAA. I could lose my license."

"It's not Julie I want to talk to you about," Tucker said. "It's Zach Burns."

"Excuse me?" The doctor frowned.

"I looked at the medical records associated with Wynona Burns' death," Tucker said. "You were asked to give Zach Burns a psychological evaluation after his mother died, and I was wondering why a GP would be asked to provide such an evaluation."

"For one thing, I was Zach Burns' primary physician," he replied. "For another, I wasn't always a GP, as you call it. I was... well, that's in the past. Ask your questions, Mr. Randall. I'll answer them if I can."

Tucker glanced at Linda. She obviously wasn't happy. "Is there somewhere we can talk in private?" he asked.

"Of course. We'll go to my office. If you'll follow me?"

"Please, sit down," Wilson said when they entered his office. "It's not very grand, I'm afraid, but it serves my needs."

Tucker glanced at the piles of paper on his desk. *So, he really is doing paperwork. Maybe I read it wrong... Nah. Those two have something going. I'm sure of it.*

"So, how can I help you?" Wilson said, clasping his hands together on the desk.

"What can *you* tell me about Zach Burns?" Tucker asked.

Wilson frowned. "Off the top of my head, and after all these years, not much, I'm afraid. Let's see..." He leaned back in his chair and stared up at the ceiling. "Zach Burns? Hmm. He was in the house the night his mother was brutally murdered. He received a blow to the head and was in a state of semi-consciousness when he was found. He spent a day at Memorial, then was taken into custody and questioned, but he was unable to provide any answers other than he couldn't remember anything. That was when Sheriff Cundiff asked me to take a look at him, which I did."

"So what you're telling me is that he lost his memory?" Tucker asked.

"In a nutshell, yes and no. Dissociative amnesia," Wilson replied. "At first, everyone, like you, believed that he'd 'lost his memory,'" he said with a smile. "He didn't. That's a terrible misunderstanding of the problem. Dissociative amnesia occurs when a person blocks out certain events, often associated with stress or trauma, leaving the person unable to remember important personal information; the memory, however, but for the odd gaps, such as the several hours during which Burns either murdered his mother or watched it happen, remains intact. That's the layman's definition."

He paused for a moment before continuing, "Zach had one or more heavy blows to the head, and I think he probably watched his mother being... murdered. It's likely he blacked out from the physical trauma and then willed himself to forget the terrible events he witnessed. Other than the gap, his memory is as it always was, intact."

"What happened after he was released?" Tucker asked.

"Wynona's sister, Angela Sidenham, I believe her name was, took him in. He lived with her until he graduated high school—a little more than two years—during which I saw him twice, I think, but his condition hadn't changed, and it probably never will. Anyway, as I said, he graduated high school, and less than three months later, he disappeared into the forest—that would have been... thirteen years ago?—and little has been seen of him since."

"The rumors are that there was no second person,"

Tucker said. "That he killed his mother and received his injuries in the process."

The doctor shook his head. "No. I don't think so. I'm afraid some of the local folks started that rumor. But after the incident with his football coach, it became a full-blown truth, if you know what I mean." Wilson steepled his fingers and looked at him across his desk. "I tend to go with the evidence, and, by all accounts, there was none."

"Yes, I heard about the incident with his coach," Tucker replied. "I'm surprised he wasn't expelled."

"He probably would have been had the coach not taken up for him and admitted he pushed him a little too hard."

Tucker tried not to think of Burns' size, his quickness, or his ability to disappear into the forest. But like the doctor, he believed in the evidence, and the lack of a body or murder weapon were pretty conclusive. *Zach Burns did not kill his mother.*

"So, is Zach Burns considered a suspect?" Wilson asked.

"More a person of interest," Tucker said.

"I understand," Wilson said. "Well, I hope I was able to answer your questions, Mr. Randall. But I really do need to get back to my paperwork." He spread his arms as if to encompass the stacks of paper on his desk. "If not, I'll be here all night. So, if there's nothing else."

"Of course," Tucker replied. "Thank you for taking the time and for allowing me to barge in here like I did. I don't think Ms. Warner was too happy about it, though."

"She's very protective of me," Wilson said as he walked him back to the reception area. "Show Mr. Randall out, please, Mrs. Warner. And you can lock up and go yourself."

"Yes, Doctor," she replied, rising from her seat and gathering her things.

Mrs. Warner, Tucker thought. *No wonder she didn't want to call the police.*

CHAPTER 23

"One more thing, Mr. Randall," Wilson said as he was about to step outside. "I still need your paperwork."

"Yes, I'm sorry," Tucker replied. "I guess it slipped my mind. I'll get it to you ASAP. Goodnight, Doctor."

Wilson nodded, turned away and disappeared back into the labyrinth.

24

SUNDAY EVENING 6:15PM

Mallory was in one of those moods when she arrived home a little before five that Sunday afternoon. She was tired, elated, and disappointed, all at the same time. Tired for obvious reasons, elated because Tucker had "welcomed her to the team," and disappointed that he hadn't taken her with him to the sheriff's department.

So, when she arrived home loaded up with groceries and Julie's laptop, she let Annie out and quickly loaded the groceries into the refrigerator. Then she poured herself a huge glass of red, took a big gulp, closed her eyes, swallowed, shuddered, then opened the door to let Annie back in.

She stood for a moment at the open door, looking out toward the distant mountains, and again she shuddered; this time thinking about her encounter with Zach Burns and then at the thought of what might have happened to Julie.

Finally, she stepped back inside and closed the door,

picked up the laptop and, glass in hand, carried it into the living room, sat down in her recliner, put up her feet, set the laptop on her knees and opened it. Then, having set her glass down on the side table, she put her head back and closed her eyes.

An hour and a half later, she opened her eyes again with a start, looked at the dark computer screen, then around the room. *Oh Lord,* she thought. *I must have fallen asleep again.* And then she realized she was hungry. So she set the computer aside, struggled out of the recliner, and went to the kitchen.

For a moment, she wondered what Tucker was doing and whether to invite him over for something to eat—but decided against it.

So, she thought, *I'm on the team. I wonder what that means... exactly? Hah. Not a whole lot, if I'm honest with myself. I'm out of a job, have just enough money set aside to carry me through the next three months... and no prospects. Damn. Oh well, I do have the laptop, and I can look through the messages by myself. Phew.* She blew out a huge breath and sat down at the kitchen table. *I've been feeling so tired lately, and I've been eating nothing but garbage. I need to do better. I must have put on five or ten pounds, and I look like hell. I need to get back on my diet and burn off the fat.*

She turned her head and looked at the fridge, grinned and muttered, "I'll start tomorrow."

Annie looked up at her, head tilted to one side.

"Oh, don't look at me like that," she said to the dog. "I'll start tomorrow. I promise."

"Errrr, woof."

"Oh shut up, Annie," she said, getting up from the table and going to the fridge.

She opened the freezer section and stared inside without enthusiasm. For a moment, she considered ordering a pizza but decided she couldn't wait. So she grabbed a bag of Orange Chicken from Trader Joe's and some microwavable Jasmine rice, and less than fifteen minutes later, she and Annie were enjoying the pseudo-Chinese delight.

Now, she thought, having rinsed off her plate and Annie's dish and put them in the dishwasher, *let's take a look at those messages.*

She set the laptop on the kitchen table, plugged it in, and opened the Sibilant program.

The early messages to Kal had been flirty and fun, and Julie obviously enjoyed talking to him.

> **MakeLikeATree:** *18:32*
> *I love that you're out there watching over us. It makes me feel safe.*

DeputyDawg: *18:37*
You know it babe.

But the dialogue soon became strained.

Messages from Julie, for example: *I can't believe you did that,* and *Why did you lie to me?* received responses like *sorry babe you know how dad is,* or *look its confidential you know,* and *can we just talk about it?*

But then it seemed as if some messages were missing altogether, or perhaps the conversations had continued off-screen. And Mallory began to think she was missing key information. And then the messages stopped for several months until Julie had a minor car accident, a fender-bender that Julie had never mentioned, not to her or her mother because Jennifer would have told her about it. It was then that the messaging resumed.

MakeLikeATree: *19:54*
Look, I just don't want my parents finding out, ok?
I wasn't supposed to be out there tonight

DeputyDawg: *19:57*
sure babe you know i can do anything for you
can we let the past be past?
Just go out with me again ok

MakeLikeATree: *20:01*
I can't change the fact that you do what you do
and I can't forget about it

DeputyDawg: *20:03*
im not saying you have to forget
but you dotn need to make
a big deal out of it
its nothing

MakeLikeATree: *20:05*
You're a cop and you're breaking the law, Kal.
What kind of person are you Doing that kind of stuff?
It's wrong, and I can't be involved. It's not right.

DeputyDawg: *20:06*
Oh come Jules aint you been asking me to break the law

CHAPTER 24

*a little? You know im
protecting you give me
another chance please*

MakeLikeATree: *20:08*
*Fine. I'll go out with you,
just for a drink. Nothing more
But you have to stop.*

DeputyDawg: *20:12*
*great. but change your screen name
pick something nice again*

Ariel: *20:16*
How's this?

DeputyDawg: *20:19*
*awesome. like the mermaid
you gonna wear any seashells for ne?*

Ariel: *20:20*
*Only if a storm strands us on a
deserted island*

DeputyDawg: *20:21*
*thats ok
i like how you look without
anything on anyway*

"Oh... my God," Mallory muttered, shuddering at the thought of Kal and Julie naked together. "That totally creeps me out. Whatever was she thinking?" *And what was she thinking, going back to him after... whatever it was? I guess she must have found out that Kal was involved with the moonshiners. What was it Tucker said?* "You think you know someone, but you really don't," she muttered. *Geez, did I ever really know Julie? And how weird is it that she found Zach, who thought of himself as an ogre—*

Her phone beeped, startling her.

"What the heck?" she said as she picked it up and looked at the screen. It was a text.

Oil Points Bulletin *18:25*

Have you checked your mileage lately?

Be sure to stop into your local Oil Baron—

"Geez, like I needed a panic attack," Mallory muttered as she marked it spam.

"Pheeew," she said and made a noise with her lips. "Oil Points Bulletin..." *Didn't Kal say they put one of those out for Julie's Bronco? Not oil, though, all points bulletin. Crap.* She shook her head. *You've got to stop this, Mallory. Not everything has to be about the case, does it? Geez, it seems as if Julie's occupying your every waking thought. Of course she would. You love her. Why wouldn't she?*

But Mallory was tired, really tired. She'd been fighting the system for more than two weeks. Between work and the searching and the digging, she'd barely slept a wink, and on top of all that, she'd been neglecting her health, lost her job, and was probably looking at a lawsuit. She just wanted it to be over.

But it won't ever be over. Not unless we prove that she went missing, or she ran away, or she's dead. We'll always wonder.

But the thought of the All Points Bulletin nagged at her. *When did the sheriff's department post the APB? How far out did*

CHAPTER 24

that range? Ten miles? Twenty? Fifty? A hundred? Lordy, that's a big area.

"I wonder if they still have the APB active?" she muttered. "I bet they don't. They weren't interested in looking for her right from the start. I wonder if they heard anything, and if they did, did they follow up on it? I bet they didn't. Damn that Kal Cundiff. I wish I could…"

Okay, so let's take the positive approach, she thought. *I can do some checking myself, but where? Hmm, I know. Tucker mentioned salvage yards. That's a good place to start.*

She Googled "salvage and scrap yards near me." That brought up more than a dozen listings in the Chattanooga area alone.

She opened a Notepad document and copied and pasted the names of the businesses into a document. She stared at it for a moment, then had another thought: *I need to widen the search. Suppose I stole a car in Ocoee. Where would I take it? Probably not Chattanooga. Hmm. Okay, so how about East Tennessee?*

She Googled "auto salvage and scrap yards in east Tennessee." That brought up a single business in East Memphis. *Hmm. I'll just have to do it by county. That will take all night. Okay, so let's narrow it down, then.*

Thirty minutes later, she had listings in ten counties, including two in North Carolina.

She looked at the clock. "It's seven-forty… and Sunday. I'll have to start in the morning."

She looked at Annie, who was asleep in her bed. "Come on, girl. I'll take you out, then we'll make it an early night."

Annie jumped up and ran to the back door.

Mallory stepped out onto the back deck and sat down in an Adirondack chair to watch Annie do her stuff.

You know, she thought as she watched the dog disappear into the long grass at the far end of the garden, *it probably doesn't matter if I call them tonight. I mean, I could leave messages and they could call me back in the morning. That might even be better. I could get them all done tonight instead of talking to each and every one; that would save a lot of time.*

She stood up. "Annie," she called. "Come on. We have work to do." And the dog came running up the garden path.

"Good girl," Mallory said, bending down and making a fuss of her. "You want a treat?" Annie wagged her tail furiously. "Of course you do. Come on then."

She gave the dog a Meaty Bone, then settled down in her recliner and looked at her Notepad document. "That's not going to work," she said and took five minutes to transfer the information into a spreadsheet. Then she took a deep breath and called the first name on the list. It rang twice before the voicemail picked up. She waited until the over-friendly spiel ended, then for the beep, and then she began.

"Hi, my name is Mallory Carver, and this is an urgent request as part of a homicide investigation." *Oh, dear God. I hope it isn't.* "We're looking for a missing nineteen-ninety-two Ford Bronco, tan and brown, with a crumpled passenger side front fender. It also has a lot of stickers on the tailgate. The tag number is XLT941. If you've seen this vehicle within the last three weeks, please contact me direct at this number. Thank you." She gave the number, hung up and marked it off on the spreadsheet.

That should do it, she thought as she dialed the next number on the list.

By ten after ten, she was done. She'd left messages at ninety-three businesses. She was exhausted and could barely keep her eyes open.

She'd made calls to businesses in Athens, Decatur, Evensville, Pikeville and most of east Tennessee as far north as Knoxville. She'd called companies in Georgia as far as Dalton, Ringgold, Chatsworth, Mineral Bluff, Ellijay, and even Chickamauga.

"I'm done," she mumbled. "I need to go to bed." She yawned and looked at Annie. The dog was asleep in her bed, on her back, all four legs in the air.

"Come on, Annie," she said. "One last pee-pee and we'll go night-night."

MONDAY MORNING 9:10AM

Mallory woke late the next morning, Monday, when, at just after nine o'clock, her cell phone rang, or rather buzzed on the nightstand. At first she thought it was part of her dream and ignored it, and it wasn't until it fell off onto the floor that she decided she needed to answer it.

Vision bleary, body aching, head aching, she leaned over the edge of the bed, groping for the errant phone. Finally, she found it, grabbed it and looked at the time. "Oh... m'God," she gasped as she flung herself back onto the pillow. "It's ten after nine. How did I sleep that long?"

The call ended before she could answer it. She held the phone up so she could see it and saw there were dozens of missed calls; messages. She opened her voicemail and found thirty-five new messages. "Oh shit."

"Come on, Annie," she snapped as she leaped out of bed and almost fell. "Whoops, come on, girl. You need to go out." And together, they ran down the stairs to the back door.

She turned the dog loose, then all but ran back up the stairs to the bathroom, took a quick shower, and dressed quickly in a pair of old jeans and a white T-shirt. She ran back to the bathroom, brushed her hair. Then, feeling *almost* like a new person, she ran back downstairs, peeked out the glass pane in the back door to make sure Annie was okay, then she turned and tapped the switch on the coffee maker.

That done, she took her phone from her pocket, grabbed a paper and pen, and started playing the messages.

"Hi, this is Susie at Bucks for Trucks. I just wanted to let you know that we haven't seen any vehicles matching your description in the last three months. Hope your search goes well."

She wrote *BFTrucks — no*.

She played the next message. "Hi, this is Eric from Olympic Towing. Haven't seen anything like that. Sorry."

She wrote *Olympic — no*.

She heard Annie scratching at the door to come in. She let her in, refreshed her coffee, then went back to work.

She played the next message, the next, and the next, all with similar messages. No one had seen the Bronco.

Diligently, she listened to each and every call until, by ten o'clock, she'd finished, feeling utterly defeated and realizing the flaw in her reasoning the night before. *What about the ones that didn't call back? Now I have to call them all again. Damn it.*

"Geez, thirty-five and nothing," she mumbled. "That leaves… fifty-eight that I have to call again." Her phone buzzed. "Please, please, please," she muttered as she accepted the call.

"Hello," she said.

"Is this Ms. Carver?"

"It is," she replied carefully, having been the victim of more spam calls than any human being deserved.

"Oh, good. Good morning. This is Derrick from B&L

CHAPTER 24

Salvage returning your call. That Bronco you're looking for? We got it. It ain't in good shape, though."

"Oh, my Lord, thank you, Derrick," she replied. "How long have you had it?"

"It came in about a week ago. It's been stripped. Had to be hauled in. It's scheduled for crushing, but—"

"Oh, please, don't do that," Mallory said, her heart thudding. "It's evidence in a possible murder case. Can you send me a picture of it? Just to be sure? I need to see it."

"Sure. Give me a second—" It wasn't thirty seconds later that she received a message. She opened the file to see a picture of a computer screen on which was a photograph of Julie's Bronco: the familiar front grill and headlights, the minor crumple on the passenger side fender. *Oh, my God. That's it,* she thought. *That's Julie's Bronco.*

"That's it," she said, unable to contain her excitement. "Does it have stickers all over the tailgate?"

"Not that I know of," Derrick replied, "but to be honest, I didn't look. You sure this is the one you're looking for?"

"Yes. I'm sure," she replied. "What's the tag number?"

"No Tag. Plate's missing. Sorry."

"Okay. Not a problem. I'm coming to look at it. Please don't do anything to it. Where's your shop, or yard, or… Where are you?"

"Like I said, lady, it ain't in the best con—"

"It doesn't matter. Where are you, sir?"

"We're in Maryville"—he pronounced it Murvul—"off of Highway 411."

"Could you give me the address, please, for my GPS?" she asked.

"Sure," he said and gave her the address.

"Hold on, please," she said.

She went to her laptop on the kitchen table, brought up Google Maps and tapped in the address.

"You still there, Derrick?" she asked.

"Sure am."

"It's about a two-hour drive from where I am," she said. "I'll start out as soon as I can. Will you be there around… It's almost twenty after ten now. We should be there around one, give or take. Will you be there?"

"Yup. I go to lunch around twelve, so yeah. Come at one."

Her phone buzzed in her ear, but she ignored it.

"I'm on my way," she said.

25

MONDAY MORNING 9:30AM

At nine-fifteen that morning, Tucker was seated in his car a half block down the street from Dr. Wilson's clinic, wondering if he'd missed her and whether or not he should go inside. He'd been there since seven-forty-five, hoping to catch Linda Warner on her way in to work.

Why? Because he had a hunch, a gut feeling that something wasn't quite right about the so-called good doctor. Was it something the man had said to him or the way he'd said it? Or the way he'd spoken to Mallory? He didn't know. What he did know was that the feeling wouldn't go away until he'd figured out what it was that was bothering him.

Tucker was a seasoned investigator taught his craft by the best in the business, and he'd long ago learned to trust his feelings; thus, he listened to his hunches, and he wasn't alone. There was something indefinable about a hunch, and every lawman in any capacity learned early on to "trust their gut."

And Tucker Randall's gut was telling him there was something decidedly iffy going on at Dr. Wilson's little clinic.

Dr. Wilson had been more than willing to talk about Mallory while he was stitching Tucker's arm, weaving a subtle tale of a girl always on the lookout for adventure, getting into trouble and not always telling the truth. *Sure, Mallory comes across as excitable sometimes,* he thought and slowly shook his head. *But she's not a liar.*

His gut told him that much, and she'd proved herself a meticulous, though occasionally emotional, temporary partner. *And why wouldn't she be emotional about her missing niece?*

Then he'd asked Wilson about Zach Burns, and the doctor's readiness to talk about him in spite of the HIPAA laws—which had been the first thing he'd mentioned when he told him he wanted to ask him some questions—was just one more twitch in his gut. A twitch that had grown and festered after he, the doctor, had painted a portrait of a gruff and brutal teenager who'd turned to violence, and perhaps even murder, matricide. *But bitter and violent men, and especially murderers, don't serve tea to trespassers. And it sure as hell didn't take much persuasion to get the doctor to talk about him, regardless of his supposed fear of the aforementioned HIPAA laws... But above all, I just don't like the man. He's one snide, arrogant...*

He dismissed the thought from his mind. His personal feelings about the doctor were irrelevant. He'd seen the doctor arrive at eight, followed a moment later by his nurse, but of Linda Warner, there had been no sign. *So,* he thought. *I've either missed her or she's not at work today... Nope, that's her red Honda Civic over there in the corner of the lot, so she must have come in early. Oh well. Can't sit around here all day. Let's go talk to her, Tucker.*

CHAPTER 25

He was reaching for the starter button when he saw the clinic door open. Expecting it to be a patient, he started the engine and was about to put the car in drive when Linda Warner scurried out. He touched the button again and turned off the engine. Then he checked the dashboard clock. It was nine-thirty exactly.

"A little early for lunch," Tucker muttered, "but hey, I'll take what I can get."

He stepped out of the car and headed in Linda's direction. She was almost to the street corner when he caught up with her.

"Linda. Is that you? I was just on my way to the clinic. Have you got a minute?"

She stopped walking, turned and saw who it was, and she wasn't pleased. "Mr. Randall?" she said angrily. "No. I don't want to talk to you." And she turned again and began to walk quickly away.

He quickened his pace and caught up with her again. "Wait, Linda. Just hold on a minute, please?" he said, hoping the familiarity of his use of her first name would give her pause. "I just want to ask a few questions... about a missing girl—"

"I know what you want," she said furiously, interrupting him. And without slowing her pace, she continued, "And I told you I don't want to talk to you. Now go away and leave me alone. D'you hear?"

Tucker followed her around another corner. "Listen to me, please? I just want to ask you about Julie Romero. She's missing, and her family is distraught. She was Doctor Wilson's patient. I just want to find the girl."

"Then why are you bothering the doctor?" she demanded, still marching onward, her head down, eyes staring straight ahead.

"I really don't know the answer to that, Linda. Julie was

his patient. I'm just looking for a little insight into the girl's... I don't know... character? I want to find her and put her parents' minds at rest. If you'll just give me a minute and answer a few questions, I promise I'll leave both you and the good doctor alone. How does that sound?"

Linda slowed to a walk, then to a stop, turned around, looked him in the eye and said, "D'you mean that? Because Doctor John says you're just looking for a camera opportunity and some dirty laundry to air."

"He said what?" Tucker asked, stunned by the revelation. "I promise you, that's the last thing I want to do."

He watched her features soften, then, "Now you listen to me, Mr. Randall." She lowered her head and stared up at him through her lashes while wagging a finger at him. "John Wilson is a wonderful man."

"I'm sure he is—" Tucker replied.

"He does a lot for this community," she said, cutting him off again, "and I'm not going to let you ruin him."

"I understand, and that's not my intention," Tucker replied.

"And his wife is a harridan, a shrew. I don't care what anyone else thinks about the Burns family." She drew herself up.

What? Where the hell did that come from?

"Stasia doesn't appreciate him, hasn't for years. But he's trapped in a prenup that would destroy him. Ever since the misunderstanding that got him dismissed from Erlanger, he's been completely dependent on his wife for money."

What the hell is she talking about?

"He's married to a member of the Burns family?" Tucker asked, stunned.

"Yes, Stasia Burns," she replied. "She pays for almost everything."

"But, what about his practice? Surely—"

Again, she cut him off. "Oh, his clinic hardly makes enough money to stay open. And he's a very generous man, you know. He donates to all sorts of good causes, helps troubled families in the community. He even gives free therapy sessions at night." She was obviously upset.

"Linda, what did I do last night to upset you?" he asked gently.

"Why, you... You came in and disturbed him while he was doing his essential paperwork. Sunday is the only time he can do it. And I really should have locked the door, but as usual, he'd agreed to see Mrs. Adams for an unscheduled therapy session. That's the kind of man he is. I was afraid he'd—"

"Be angry with you for letting me in?" Tucker asked.

"No. Not angry," she said, looking around to see if anyone was nearby. "It was... I... That is, we... I didn't want him to be upset."

Tucker looked at her. Her eyes were watering. "You two... You're..." He didn't want to say it, but on the other hand, he wanted to know.

Linda lowered her head and her voice. "My husband, you see, Walter, passed away five years ago. It's been very difficult for me. He was a good man and I miss him, but..." She looked up at him and shrugged. "Well, you know."

Wow, Tucker thought. *What do I say to that?* "Yes, of course. I understand—"

And, yet again, she cut him off. "I'm fifty-three, Mr. Randall. No one wants to... It's hard to find..." She bit her lip. "No one wants to date a fifty-three-year-old secretary, and he... Well, sometimes after work... he and I, we... Oh, my God. You know what I mean. So when you burst in and he got upset and told me to leave... yes. I was pissed off. I'd been looking forward to... some time alone with him."

"I'm sorry," Tucker said. "I didn't know. Here, let me give you my card. If you think of anything about Julie, anything at all, really, please let me know."

Linda took the card from him, glanced at it, then slipped it into her purse. "I have to go now. I have to get the doctor something to eat. It's going to be a busy day. Goodbye, Mr. Randall." And she walked away, her head held high.

Tucker watched her go, walked toward his car, then turned again and watched her go into the sandwich shop. He shook his head. *Unbelievable,* he thought as he opened his car door and slid in behind the wheel.

He sat for a moment thinking, wondering what to do next. He frowned. *Strange,* he thought. *I haven't heard from Mallory. That's not like her.*

He took out his phone and called her. It went directly to voicemail.

"Hi. I'm not available right now. Leave a message—"

He ended the call, frustrated. *Damn it! What the hell is she doing?*

He dropped the phone onto the passenger seat and reached for the starter button, and the phone rang. He glanced at it. *Hah! It's Mallory.*

"Hey. I just called you."

"Yeah. I know. Sorry. I was—Oh, never mind. You need to get over here right away. We've got to go."

"Go? What are you talking about? Go where?" Tucker asked.

"I found Julie's Bronco," she yelped.

"Geez," he replied, pushing the starter. "How did you do that? Where is it?"

"I made some calls. It's in Maryville. It's about two hours away, so come on."

CHAPTER 25

Some thirty minutes later, after a heated argument about who would drive—which Tucker lost decisively—they were on I-75 driving north in Mallory's Dodge Ram pickup.

Why do I get the feeling that she could have solved this case all by herself? he wondered as they rocketed through the I-75/I-24 split. *She's like a dog with a bone; never gives up.*

But he also remembered the rack of destroyed wine bottles at The Saloon and the way she yelled at Zach Burns, a man twice her size. *And a frickin' big dog, at that, and I sometimes wonder if she's not all...*

"So, what did you find out this morning?" Mallory asked, breaking into his thoughts without taking her eyes from the road, and as she reached out to adjust the radio to a classic country music station.

"D'you mind?" Tucker said, changing it to a soft rock station. "I'm not a fan of country music."

She glanced at him and frowned. "Really?"

"Yes, really," he replied. "It's all... 'my girl left me, my momma died, someone stole my truck.' It's depressing, a mood killer."

"Hah!" she said and shook her head. "So, are you going to tell me or not?" she asked.

"I found... Look, I'm not sure it's worth sharing."

"What do you mean?" Mallory said. "You haven't had a problem sharing anything else."

"I just mean... I'm not sure it means anything. And... Oh hell. Doctor Wilson is having an affair with his secretary, Linda Warner."

"What?" She whipped her head around to look at him, and the truck veered violently to the right onto the edge of the hard shoulder.

"See?" he said as she eased the big vehicle back onto the pavement. "That's exactly the reaction I expected. I told you. It doesn't mean anything. Now keep your eyes on the road, *please.*"

Mallory was sullenly silent for a while, and Tucker couldn't help but wonder, *What's going on in that pretty little head of yours?* But he settled back in his seat, closed his eyes and said nothing.

"You know, it's going to be a really boring ride if all I have to talk about is the number of phone calls I made last night." Mallory shifted in her seat. "So what else can we talk about?"

"You seem to be obsessed with your true-crime podcasts and talk about them all the time, so I'm told," Tucker said. "Why do you listen to that crap? It's beyond depressing… and it's unhealthy."

"That's enthusiasm, not obsession," she countered. "And where was this hesitation to speak when Cundiff told you about his smuggling operation?"

"That pertained to the case, and I was hoping to learn something," Tucker said, then paused and continued. "And what about that shouting match you had with your boss? And the stunt you pulled with the liquor rack?"

"Former boss," she said, smiling. "He's a horse's ass and I have no regrets. Hell, I enjoyed it." She paused, then continued quietly, "Maybe the booze thing was a little over the top."

"Thank you," Tucker said, closing his eyes again. "I should have left you behind and done this myself. Now stop being so annoying and concentrate on your driving."

"You couldn't have left me behind because I'm the only one who can identify her Bronco."

"Really?" he said. "Nineteen-ninety-two model, tan and brown, crumpled passenger side front fender, stickers all over the tailgate. How many of those can there be in East Tennessee?"

"Geez," she muttered. "All right. You win. Satisfied?"

Tucker smiled but didn't answer.

Mallory drove on in silence until they reached Athens and then said, "You said you were in the FBI, and then you quit after the girl died, right?" Mallory asked quietly. "So why did you become a private investigator?"

Tucker pursed his lips, looked at her and said, "It wasn't just the Marsha Cline case. She was just the beginning of the end. I've never quite gotten over her; probably never will… Okay, so it wasn't long after she died when a little boy went missing.

"I told David, my boss, I could do the job. I wanted to prove to myself—and maybe to David, too—that I was still the agent I should be. Anyway, I approached the family and discovered the boy had an uncle. To cut a long story short, it turned out the uncle's friend was the perp. I tracked him down, arrested him, found where he had the kid locked up, and then made the mistake of talking to the media. Then I was handed another missing person case—are you beginning to see a pattern here? It turned out that she, the mother, had ditched her family and run off with another guy. It took a while, but I found her and again, I ended up on TV."

He sighed. "And one case followed another, all missing persons, kidnappings, murders, six more cases, and I just got fed up with the interviews and the publicity. And all the time, Marsha was there, haunting me, playing with my mind. And then, one day, I bumped into the Clines in the mall, and Jim Cline told me in no uncertain terms that I was a grandstanding jerk, bragging about how many cases I'd solved. That was it. That was all it took. I quit the FBI, applied for a PI license, and swore I'd never take another missing person case as long as I lived."

"But you took our case," Mallory said. "Why?"

He shrugged. "I think I told you before, your sister shoved that photo of Julie under my nose. I thought for a minute it was Marsha. So, I took it as a sign from above that maybe I could make amends for my past failures. It's not going too well, is it?"

He lapsed into silence, leaned his head back against the rest, hands on his knees and closed his eyes.

It was no more than a moment later when he felt Mallory's hand close over his. She gave it a gentle squeeze and then took her hand away and put it back on the wheel, and said, "It will be all right, Tucker. We'll find her. I know we will."

But he didn't know if she'd be alive when they did.

26

MONDAY AFTERNOON 6PM

Mallory spent the rest of the ride to Maryville trying to decide what to say to Tucker, but she could never find the right words.

And none of the things I've done over the last ten years, and in particular the last three weeks, have been any help at all.

Five long days searching the trail had turned up nothing.

Her dives into Julie's phone records had missed Sarah's involvement.

She'd had no idea Julie was dating Kal Cundiff.

She'd had no idea the Cundiffs were running an illegal smuggling operation.

She'd missed the importance of Julie's laptop entirely.

She'd not known that Julie was involved with Zach Burns.

Yes, she had managed to find the Bronco, but any competent police search would have found it two weeks ago.

"This is it," Tucker said, jerking her out of her reverie. "There. Hey, Mallory. You've passed it."

She braked, looked around and saw the sign go by to the left. "Whoops. Sorry. I was... Oh never mind. Hang on," she said as she checked her mirrors. Then she made an illegal U-turn, drove back several hundred yards, made a right into the yard and parked outside the converted container that served as the office.

She jumped out of the truck, suddenly feeling quite nervous—not something she experienced very often. But this really was the moment.

"Let's do this, Tucker," she said and took a deep breath and marched into the office. "Hi," she said brightly. "Are you Derrick?"

He looked up at her, did a double take, then rose to his feet and said, "No, I'm Gus. Derrick's out in the yard. What can I do ya for?"

"I called earlier about a tan and brown Bronco. Derrick said—"

"Oh, yeah," Gus said. "That one. He told me about it."

Mallory waited for him to say something else.

"We got it," he said, finally.

"Can we see it?" Mallory asked.

"I guess," he replied. "Dunno why you'd want to, though. It's in pretty bad shape—"

"Gus," Tucker interrupted, "that Bronco may be the missing piece in a police investigation. We need to see it."

"Nah," he said, shaking his head. "The police already investigated it."

"That would have been the local police," Mallory said, her impatience mounting. "It's the subject of a police investigation. Now. Can we see it, please?"

"Whatever. It's barely salvage now," Gus muttered. He pointed to a crudely drawn map on the wall. "We're here,"

CHAPTER 26

he said. "You wanna follow along to right here, and when you get to the Jeeps—"

"Can you just show us, please? We've had a really long drive," Mallory said, pleading.

The man gave her a dismissive shrug. She drew herself up to her full height and glared at him.

He rolled his eyes and then said, "Sheesh, women! Okay, I got a few minutes. Follow me." And he led them out into the semi-chaotic structure of what turned out to be a major salvage yard, a maze of pathways bounded by stacks of scrap and crushed vehicles. They followed him as he made turn after turn following a set of landmarks that could only have made sense to him.

"Here it is," he said finally. "They found it in the parking lot at the rear of an abandoned strip mall about five miles from here. Is it yours?"

"It was my niece's," Mallory said.

"Well," Gus said, "you sure this here's the one?"

The Bronco was, indeed, Julie's. But not even Gus' previous warnings had prepared her for what she saw.

The Bronco was on its axles. The wheels were missing, and so was the license plate. The outside of the body was pretty much as Mallory remembered it, but the interior had been completely stripped, picked clean. But it was the tailgate that upset her the most.

Julie had been an avid sticker collector. Wherever she went, she would buy a sticker for her tailgate. Mallory had helped her put the first ones on when she was only sixteen. Jared had bought the car for her sixteenth birthday, and by the time she was twenty-three, the tailgate was entirely covered. To look at it from behind, you couldn't tell what color it was.

But now, all the stickers were gone. Someone had taken the time to remove them all. Not a trace of Julie remained.

And she realized that any hope she might have had that Julie was alive, this deliberate attempt to erase her presence from the Bronco, made it clear that someone had wanted her to disappear.

"I need to get the VIN number," Tucker said. "You said it was found at the rear of a strip mall," he continued. "It was taken from a parking area at a trailhead off of Highway 64 in the Cherokee National Forest more than two weeks ago. That's quite a haul from here. And it was brought in… when, exactly?"

Gus frowned, narrowed his eyes, thought for a moment, then said, "Not sure exactly when. Not without checking the log, but I'm thinking… it was a week ago Friday, late afternoon, as I remember it. Tow guy said the cops had called it in. Chased some kids away from it. You're lucky it's still here. It was scheduled for the crusher this morning."

So convenient, Mallory thought. *Just some kids playing in an abandoned car. No wonder the cops didn't bother with it.*

Tucker turned to Mallory and said, "We need to call this in to Sheriff Cundiff. I wonder where it was the week before it was found? Someone went to a lot of trouble to make sure it couldn't be identified. Several of the VIN numbers have been removed, even the one on the engine, but whoever it was missed the one on the inside of the tailgate. I've made a note of it. I'll call it in when we're done here."

Mallory said nothing. She could only stare at the ruined vehicle.

"I need the address where the Bronco was found," Tucker said to Gus. "Maybe we can get some camera footage."

"Again, I'll need to check the log," Gus replied. "We can

do that now. I need to go back to the office anyway. You done here, miss?"

"I'll be a minute," she replied. "I need to take some photos. You go on. I'll catch up."

"Don't be long," Tucker said. "We have a long drive back."

She nodded, took her phone from her pocket and took as many photos as she could of the interior, front, back, and driver's side. She couldn't get to the passenger side because the car was pushed up against a stack of crushed vehicles more than two stories high.

That done, she walked back to the office, wondering how she was going to tell Jen and Jared that Julie was almost certainly dead. It was a thought that almost made her throw up.

Is this what Tucker felt like? she wondered. *If he did... if he does, I can understand why. This is the worst moment of my life, and it's not even over.*

By the time she reached the office, she could barely hold back the tears. She arrived just in time to hear Tucker hand over his phone to a man she didn't recognize standing next to Gus. He turned out to be the elusive Derrick, the yard manager.

"Sheriff Cundiff would like to talk to you," Tucker said as he handed Derrick his phone.

"This is Derrick Sims," he said.

There was a pause while he listened.

"Yes, sir, Sheriff. I'll get right on it." He nodded his head.

"Yes, sir. I'll need a warrant." He put his hand over the phone and whispered to Gus. "Go rope that Bronco off and put a sign on it. It's not to be touched." He waved for Gus to go right away.

"Sorry," Derrick said into the phone. "I was just telling

my foreman to rope it off. You need me to organize transport for you?"

He winced when he heard what could only have been a negative response.

"Okay, okay," he said. "I got it. It's not to be touched. So when—" Derrick stopped talking abruptly and listened, his mouth hanging open.

"We close at six," he said, shaking his head.

"Yeah. Yeah. No... Fine, but somebody's going to have to pay for my time. Yeah. Uh, uh, no. Okay. By ten o'clock... Yeah. Yeah. And goodbye to you, too, Sheriff." Derrick let out a low whistle.

"Geez," he said as he handed the phone back to Tucker. "Is he always like that?"

Tucker grinned at him. "The guy doesn't take no for an answer."

"You can say that again," Derrick replied. "He's sending a flatbed from the Chattanooga forensic department. Said he'll call me back with a definite time. I told him by ten. That didn't go down well." He sighed and shook his head. "I promised I'd stay here and help them load it. Good thing we have good lighting. Oh well."

Tucker looked at Mallory, saw the state she was in and said, "Let's get you home, Mallory."

She nodded, thanked Derrick for calling her back and for agreeing to stay for the forensic team, and then she numbly followed him out to her truck.

"You want me to drive?" he asked.

She almost said yes, but then realized he wasn't a stick shift driver and smiled and shook her head.

"No. I'm fine," she said. "It's just... I was wondering what and how I was going to tell Jen, and it upset me, is all."

CHAPTER 26

It was a long and quiet drive back home. Neither one of them had much to say, and Mallory was glad of the quiet, but when she pulled into her driveway, Tucker looked at her and said, "Look, I don't want to come off as pushy, but I know this is a tough moment. So would you like me to call your sister for you, or is there a friend you could invite over? I'm not sure you should be alone right now."

"No. Thank you, Tucker," she replied wearily. "I'm okay. It's just that... Everything in my life is a shambles. I feel like such a total failure," she said. "Julie's gone, and I know deep in my heart that she's dead. And I don't know what to do. It's like... where do I go from here?"

Tucker let out a deep breath. "I'm so sorry, Mallory," he said, reaching out to touch her hand briefly. "Under the circumstances, I don't know what else we could have done, but I want you to understand something. Can you look at me for a second?"

She turned her head and looked at him.

"You did everything you possibly could," he said gently. "For five days, you searched the forest. You found Julie's Bronco. You found and organized all the information that we used to get us to this point. You... are amazing."

"And what good was it all?" she asked, turning her head away.

"If it wasn't for you," he insisted, "we wouldn't be where we are now. Julie disappeared without a trace. I mean... *without a trace!*"

"And now it's too late to do anything," she muttered.

"No. You're wrong," he said.

She looked back at him. His face was set.

"*I'm* not going to quit," he said. "I didn't start this, but I sure as hell am going to finish it." He hesitated for a second, then continued, "And you've been a huge help. Will you work with me a little longer?"

She shrugged. "I don't know, Tucker. I need to sleep on it. Maybe in the morning... I don't know," she repeated. "I'll need to think about it. Julie's dead. I knew that more than a week ago, but I ignored it. I knew Julie didn't run away."

She opened the car door and paused. "But thanks for all you've done and for your kind words. You're..." She closed her eyes and shook her head. "You're the first person to take me seriously in a very long time." And, not knowing what else to say, she closed the door and walked up onto her porch, hesitated at the screen, then turned and watched Tucker go to his car and drive away. She didn't notice the dilapidated pickup parked at the side of her house. Neither did Tucker.

She heaved a sigh, turned again to the screen door, opened it and heard barking in the kitchen.

"Annie," she called. "It's me. I'm home. What is it? Why are you barking?" she said as she walked into the kitchen to find the dog at the back door.

"What the..." She pushed open the back door. Annie rushed past her. She flipped on the outside light and saw Zach Burns lying face down on the deck.

"Help me," he slurred.

"Oh, my God. What happened?" she shouted as she dropped to her knees beside him. "Annie. Get away. Go on, move. Go!" Then she looked down at Zach and saw all the blood.

"Wait, wait, wait," she cried as she jumped to her feet and ran into the house to get some towels. *No, not towels!* she thought. *Too absorbent. They'll suck the blood out.* She rummaged around in her utility room, found some clean rags and grabbed a roll of packing tape. It was all she could think of.

She ran back outside, dropped to her knees beside him and said, "Zach. I need you to sit up, okay?" as she tried to lift the big man. Somehow—she never did know how—she managed to get him upright. As he leaned back against the deck rail, she opened his shirt and covered the wounds—five tiny punctures to the chest—with a pad made from the rags.

"Zach," she said, "I need you to hold it in place, tightly, while I tape it, okay?"

He placed his enormous hand over the rags as she fought to get the packing tape to unroll, then she reached around him—he was so big she could barely make it—grabbed the end of the tape with one hand and unrolled it with the other, taping his shirt and the pad of rags in place.

"Take your hand away," she said.

Weakly, he pulled his hand out from under his shirt and let it drop to his side.

"Hold up your hands, both of them, up, up. That's it. Now then," she said, as she wrapped the entire roll around his massive chest.

"Now, we need to call an ambulance and get you to a hospital—" she began.

"No" he shouted. Mallory, startled, took two steps back. "No hospital," he whispered.

"Zach, you're hurt bad," she said. "You've lost a lot of blood. We need to get you help."

"No... hospitals," he gasped. "No... hospitals."

Oh, my God. What am I going to do?

Maybe I could drive him to the ER at Erlanger, pretending that... No, that won't work. If he sees something he doesn't like, he might try to fight me while I'm driving, or jump out and run away.

"Okay, no hospitals," she agreed. "But I know someone who can help. Can I take you somewhere to get help?"

"Who to?" Zach asked.

"Someone I know. I trust him." She looked at her watch. It was almost five. "There's still time," she muttered to herself. "Come on," she said and grabbed his arm and lifted, trying to support him. "You're going to have to help me, Zach. You're too big for me to lift."

His face flickered through a series of emotions, none of which Mallory could decipher, until finally he nodded and said, "Okay." He gasped. "Julie likes you. She said she trusts you."

Somehow, she managed to get him through the house, down the porch steps and into the passenger seat. Then she ran around the truck and hopped in behind the wheel. It was only then that she noticed her white top was covered in blood.

Oh, my God, she thought for the umpteenth time as she turned the key, fired up the motor, rammed the gearshift into reverse and careened backward out onto the highway. *What the hell could have happened to him?*

"Zach," she said, glancing at him as she drove west on East Brainerd Road. "Look at me. What happened? Who shot you?"

"Don't know," he replied. "Poacher in the woods, maybe. I was looking for turkey. I didn't see him. He just shot me. I fell down. Got up. Ran. Came to find you. Only one I trust."

She thought about the blood on her back deck and shuddered. "What did he shoot you with, a shotgun?"

He was silent for a few moments, sucking in air, then he said, "Yeah. I think so. He only got me a little. I'll be alright."

She glanced sideways at him. He didn't look alright.

CHAPTER 26

Ten minutes later, she swerved into Dr. Wilson's parking lot. It was almost six o'clock, and the lot was clear except for the doctor's Cadillac and a little Honda.

"Wait here, Zach," she said and leaped out of the truck and dashed inside.

The receptionist's desk was empty. *Where's Linda?* But she had no time to ponder that.

"Dr. Wilson," she called as she leaned just past the lobby threshold. "Dr. Wilson, help! I need some help, please."

She heard some shuffling beyond the closed door, and a clang as if something had fallen to the ground, and then the door opened and a harried-looking Dr. Wilson came out into the reception area.

"Mallory," he snapped. "I might have known. What is it you want?" he demanded, his face flushed.

"Someone's badly hurt," she said. "In my truck." She almost told him it was Zach, but knowing the prejudice that surrounded him, she thought better of it. "He's in my truck," she repeated.

The doctor paused, stared at her, and then his lips curled into a slight smile and his eyes seemed to brighten. He nodded and said, "I'll be right out. Let me just grab my..." And he turned on his heel and disappeared back the way he'd come.

She ran back out to her truck. "It's going to be okay, Zach," she said through the open window. "The doctor's on his way."

Zach merely groaned in pain. His eyes remained shut.

"Zach?" she said, grabbing his arm through the window. "Zach. Wake up. I want you to know something, all right? Tucker and I, we found Julie's Bronco today. It... it was... Julie's dead, Zach. I just know she is. Whatever you and she had... I'm glad she found someone she cared about."

The sound of a car starting caught her attention. *Is that*

the doctor leaving? she wondered, turning to look at his car. *Why would he...* But it wasn't the doctor's car. It was the little red Honda.

"And I'm sorry I yelled at you," she continued, hoping that this wasn't the last time she would be able to say the things she needed to get off her chest. "I've just been so upset about not finding Julie. And you were really helpful. I hope... I hope that—"

"You know what I hope," a voice said behind her. "I hope this love fest isn't going to take much longer. I have things to do and places to be."

Mallory turned and found herself staring into the barrel of a pistol, and behind the pistol stood a smiling Dr. John Wilson.

"I was hoping for Tucker Randall," he said with a laugh. "But hah! You brought Zach to me instead. Hopefully, the third time will, indeed, be the charm."

27

MONDAY AFTERNOON 6PM

It was around five-thirty that afternoon when Tucker left Mallory at her home. She'd had little to say to him during the drive home from Maryville, and she had said only a little more to him other than goodbye when he left her, but he understood. And, as he drove back to his office, despite his promise to Mallory to stay on the job until the end, he somehow couldn't help but feel that he'd failed, again.

How did I fail? he thought. *You were supposed to find her, that's how, and you haven't, is how.* He shook his head. *There wasn't even a ten-percent chance, ever, that we'd find her alive. I knew that. And even Mallory said she knew that. So yeah, you failed, Tucker. Damn missing person cases; never again.*

Maybe Mallory and her supreme optimism had affected him a little. Maybe her professed certainty that she would find her niece and that everything would turn out well had persuaded him to believe it, too, at least a little.

It wouldn't take much. You wanted in the worst way to find this Marsha Cline lookalike, hale and hearty.

He finally made it back to his office, got out of his car and walked inside, feeling a little like a stranger in his own space. *I don't really want to be here, do I?* he thought, looking around. *Mallory's all torn up. Everything in her life has been ripped apart, her world turned upside down, and here I am, home alone. Screw it. I'm going for a drink.*

He turned around to leave again, but then he heard the all-too-familiar voice. "Mr. Randall?"

"Oh, hey, Debbie," he said as he turned back around. "I'm sorry. I didn't expect you to be here. Have I had any calls today?"

"Just one. But I need to tell you something. My Ben had a really bad fall yesterday."

"Oh, Debbie. I'm sorry to hear that," Tucker said. He'd met Ben several times. He was a hearty, smiling, and garrulous man who, given half a chance, would talk your ear off about whatever he'd been watching on the History Channel.

"I had to call the ambulance, and he's been at Erlanger since last night."

"But why didn't you tell me this… oh," Tucker said. "I left before you got here this morning, didn't I? But you could have called if you needed some time off."

"No, sir. I need to take more than just some time off. I need to leave, Mr. Randall. I'm sorry, but I have to resign… and I was hoping you'd let me leave at the end of the week. I'll tidy up all the loose ends and—"

"You want to resign? Because you need to take care of Ben," he said. "It must have been a really bad fall."

"They don't know if he can complete the physical therapy once the bones heal," she said.

"Oh… Debbie, I don't know what to say," he said. "Of course, I'll do whatever I can to help. You've been with me

CHAPTER 27

for too long for me to... Look, if there's anything you need, anything I can do."

"I appreciate that, Mr. Randall," she said with a tiny smile. "And I know you mean it, but I won't ask for anything unless it's absolutely necessary."

"I understand." *And that's why she didn't call me. Because she's the kind of woman who likes to deal with her problems herself. I'm going to miss her.*

"Well, visiting hours are until eight tonight," Debbie said, "and I promised I would come by. I'll see you in the morning, Mr. Randall," she said as she walked out the door.

He sighed and began to shuffle some of the papers on his desk. He was about to leave again to go for the drink he'd promised himself when his phone rang. He took it out of his pocket, looked at the screen. The number was unfamiliar. He was about to decline it when something told him not to. He frowned. *Who is this?*

"Hello, Tucker Randall speaking," he said.

"Mr. Randall?" the voice was female and somewhat familiar, but not one he recognized. "You said to call you if I thought..." the woman continued. "If I thought there was anything you should know. Well, there is."

"I'm sorry. Who am I speaking to?"

"It's Linda Warner," the voice whispered.

"Oh, yes. My apologies. It's been a long day," he said. *And she sounds very different. Where's the spunky, defensive woman I met earlier today?*

"Look," she said, "I know I was... a little upset before. And... Well, we didn't have any appointments late in the day today. And I was supposed to lock the door, and I didn't... you see?"

"Um... Mrs. Warner?" Tucker said. "I don't mean to rush you, but—"

"Fine," Linda huffed. "But I thought you ought to know

that your friend Mallory Carver came in a few minutes ago, before we'd... finished, and she was raving about someone being hurt. And John rushed out, then came back, grabbed something from his desk drawer and just told me to leave; to get my clothes on and leave."

But I just left Mallory less than forty-five minutes ago. What the hell? Who the hell, and... why didn't she call me for help?

"Thank you for calling me, Linda," Tucker said. "But why do I need to know about this?"

"Well, I was going over the new company credit card statement today," she said, "and two Saturdays ago, John used the clinic credit card to pay for an Uber. It was expensive; almost two hundred dollars. One hundred ninety-seven, to be precise."

"Why is that unusual?" Tucker asked, frowning, something at the back of his mind already tickling him.

"Because he always drives his car," she said. "He has a Cadillac. So when I asked him why he'd put it on the clinic card, he said he'd needed a ride for a couple of hours and got his cards mixed up and that I shouldn't worry about it. But I do. It's my job to worry about things like that."

And then it clicked, and Tucker suddenly realized the Bronco had been abandoned two hours away, in Maryville, and Gus at the scrapyard said it had been towed in more than a week ago.

"Where's Dr. Wilson now?" Tucker asked casually, not wanting to spook her.

"Well, I don't know. He's not at the clinic. I went back because, in my hurry to get out of there, I left my purse in the examination room. His car was there, but he wasn't. I guess he's working with Mallory and that gentleman who was in her truck," Linda replied.

"Did you see the man?" Tucker asked. "What did he look like?"

"I don't really know," she replied. "All I could see was that he looked... well, big? He was a big man."

Zach Burns? Has to be. But why did she take Zach Burns to —never mind.

"Linda, I hope you'll bear with me, but I need to ask you a very personal question," Tucker said. "Did the doctor ever take you somewhere... secluded? Somewhere where you two could be alone together?"

There was a moment of silence, and then, "Um... well... there were several different times—I don't remember exactly how many—when Stasia went on vacation without him," she said. "Well, anyway, that's when he first took me up to this little vacation cabin they have, the Burns family, that is. It's kind of small, so nobody ever uses it, at least that's what John told me. We've had some very nice weekends up there. And he seemed so happy, as if he'd spent his childhood there or something. I don't know. But that's where we went. Why d'you ask?"

"Linda, I need you to tell me exactly where that cabin is," Tucker said.

"But why—"

"Because the doctor's life might depend on me getting there in a hurry," he lied.

28

MONDAY EVENING 7:30PM

Mallory couldn't stop staring at the gun pointing at her head.

"Why are you doing this, Doctor Wilson?" she asked. "Why are you threatening Zach and me?"

"You? Because you're a nosy little busybody, Mallory Carver," Wilson snapped. "You always were a nasty little tyke. Him? I only ever meant to threaten him. He was the one who could unravel my life. If he'd just kept his mouth shut, none of this would ever have happened."

"Kept his mouth shut about what?" Mallory asked, her eyes wide with fear.

"There you go again," he snapped, glaring at her. "Just shut the hell up and… be quiet, or I'll shoot you both right here," He raised himself up, took his eyes off her for a moment, peered into the truck bed, then said, "Get that string stuff out and tie Burns' wrists together, tightly, and don't think I won't check."

He glanced around to make sure no one was watching.

"Come on, come on," he snapped. "Get him out of the truck and be quick about it."

Mallory did as she was told, helping Zach to slide out of the passenger seat. Then she took the baling twine from the truck bed and began wrapping it around Zach's wrists.

"Tightly now," Wilson snapped. "I'll be checking. I'm not one of those cartoon villains you see on TV. Tie it properly, tighter, yes, like that."

Oh, my God, Mallory thought. *He's flipped out. He's crazy.*

Mallory, not knowing what else to do, fearfully obeyed and did as she was told and tied Zach's wrists.

"Get out of the way," Wilson snapped and stepped forward and tugged at the bindings.

Seemingly satisfied, he nodded and said, "Now, you filthy animal, get in the back."

"What?" Mallory said. "He can't. He's injured. Can't you see?"

"Shut your mouth and help him. Do it *now!*" he snarled, waving the gun in her face.

"Oh dear," she muttered, taking Zach by the arm. "Come on, Zach. We have to do as he says."

Zach could barely stand, even with Mallory's help. He slipped as he tried to climb up and almost fell, but somehow she managed to get him seated on the tailgate and then watched him wriggle and squirm his way onto the truck bed where he lay breathing heavily, his shirt soaked with blood.

Wilson thrust the gun closer to Mallory's face and said, "Don't think I won't shoot you right in that pretty face. Now climb up there and tie his feet and be quick about it."

Again, Mallory did as she was told, wondering when, or if, she'd get a chance to make a grab for his gun. She was pretty sure she could take him, but she knew that one

CHAPTER 28

small slip and it could cost her her life—and Zach's. So she climbed up into the truck and tied his ankles.

"I'm sorry, Zach," she whispered. "It's going to be all right."

"Shut up," Wilson snapped. "Get back down here. Come on. Quickly now."

She'd been around guns most of her life, but this was the first time she'd ever had one pointed at her, and it unnerved her. She knew the slightest pressure on the trigger could end her life, and that if she was going to make a move, she had to be sure.

"Close the tailgate," Wilson said as he pointed the weapon at her.

Seven, maybe eight feet, she thought. *Too far to jump him and too close for him to miss.*

"Good," he said, the corners of his mouth turned down in a nasty grimace. "Now walk slowly around and get in. You're going to drive. Don't try anything or try to run. If you do, I'll shoot you dead."

He watched her every move until she'd climbed in behind the wheel, then he stepped up to the still-open passenger side door and said, "Good girl. Now put your hands on the wheel while I get in."

Mallory gripped the wheel tightly with both hands, trying to analyze his movements, watching for an opportunity to grab the gun.

"Good girl," he said as he closed the passenger door. Now," he continued, half turned in his seat so that he was facing her, the gun in his lap pointing at her, his finger on the trigger. "I want you to drive. If you cooperate, maybe I'll give you a little reward. And don't worry, I won't keep you up too late." His suggestive leer made her shiver.

"Why do you think I would cooperate with you?" she

snapped. *Oh, my God. He is. He's off his rocker. What am I going to do? My phone...*

"I need your phone, Mallory," he said as if reading her mind. "Hand it over."

"Why? Why d'you want my phone?"

"Mallory," he said gently. Then, *"Hand it over!"* he shouted.

She jumped, startled, then took out her phone and handed it across to him.

"That's a good girl," he said as he powered it off.

Hah, they can still track it, you crazy bastard.

"Now drive," he said. "Take I-75 north to Exit 20. Do *not* exceed the speed limit, and don't do any sudden braking. Go."

Mallory took a deep breath, put the truck in reverse, made a left turn, drove to Lee High, turned north to Bonnyoaks, made a right and took the ramp onto I-75 going north.

"Why did Zach need to keep his mouth shut?" she asked.

"What?" Wilson said as if waking from a dream.

"Why did he need to keep his mouth shut?"

"Why?" He glanced sideways at her. "Because I killed his mother," he said with a smile. "Sad, really," he continued reflectively. "I really enjoyed Jim Burns' little harpy. Never could understand why he knocked her up in the first place."

It was then Mallory knew he intended to kill them both. She bit her lip, and the truck sped up. *Oh, Lord. I have to do something—*

"Slow down," he snapped. "You're doing seventy-seven."

"But if you didn't like her, why sleep with her?" Mallory asked.

"Oh, don't dignify it with a word like sleep," Wilson

CHAPTER 28

scoffed. "I made her a deal. I cover up the fact that she brained her husband to death with a cast iron skillet, and she let me visit her whenever I... needed to, at her place. It's what we now call the 'family cabin,' though nobody ever goes there now, except for me—whenever I... needed to. It wasn't like Jim didn't deserve it anyway. He was a wicked little shit. And that nasty look she gave me every time..." He grinned at Mallory. "Boy, that was fun. I enjoyed having her bent around my little finger."

"But why did you kill her?" Mallory asked, trying to keep him talking while she tried to figure out a way to... *To what?* she thought. *He's a frickin' maniac. A total whack job.*

"It was her fault," he replied reflectively. "The silly bitch allowed herself to get *pregnant!*" Wilson shouted.

Mallory flinched, glanced at him and saw that, for some strange reason, he was smiling.

"She claimed it was some other man," Wilson continued, staring out through the windshield, and for a moment, Mallory considered making a grab for the gun. But then he looked at her and said, "But I knew better, you see. And if there was ever a paternity test that pointed to me, Stasia would ruin me. I'd be left with nothing." He shrugged and then continued.

"So I killed her. I cut her throat. Zach was outside in the woods, but he came back. I hit him over the head with a brass candlestick. He went down like a sack of shit. I hit him again. I thought he was dead. So I dragged Wynona's body out into the backyard, then came back for Zach. But he was gone. He must have run off into the woods. Head like a rock, that boy..."

He paused for a moment, then said, "Take Exit 20 and drive to Highway 64 and head east—"

"You're taking us to the forest," she said, interrupting him.

"I'm taking you to the family cabin," he replied. "You'll like it there. It's nice. Nobody ever goes there now, except for me." He paused again. Mallory glanced at him as she drove up the ramp and turned east onto APD-40.

"I never knew why anyone showed up out there the next day and found Zach semi-conscious. That was a puzzle I never did solve. Hmm."

What the hell am I going to do? Mallory was getting desperate. She knew if she didn't do something soon, she was going to die, or worse, be raped and then die. But somehow, she wasn't scared; just desperately trying to figure out how to get the gun away from him.

"Why didn't you kill Zach while he was still at school?" she asked, trying to keep him talking.

"Oh, I was going to, first chance I got. But you see, I was a psychiatrist back then—I have two medical degrees, you know—and, being as I was already treating him for depression, they asked me to do a psychological assessment. It was then I realized he was suffering from disassociative amnesia and—"

"And you could hardly kill him while he was in custody, could you?" Mallory asked sarcastically.

"See? You get it," he replied. "Ah, but you're disgusted. I like that... You know, my current... partner is a little lacking, shall we say? I don't suppose... No, I didn't think so. Oh well, never mind. It was just a thought."

Mallory refused to dignify that with a response. "So why didn't you kill Zach? You must have had plenty of chances over the years."

"You're right," he replied. "I really should have taken care of him a decade ago. But he never said anything until a few months ago; back before Christmas, it was. I thought he'd forgotten all about it, but I was out walking one of the trails and I heard someone shout, 'You killed my mother.' I looked around and saw him. I went after him, but he disappeared into the woods; good thing too, because if I'd caught him, he probably would have killed me. After that, I always carried my twelve-gauge shotgun with me."

"Then what happened?" Mallory asked. "Why now?"

"The second time I saw him, I heard a sneeze and then an arrow hit the tree next to my head. My turn to run," he said with a grin. "I caught sight of him a couple of times after that, but he always managed to get away, until yesterday afternoon, that is. I ran across him on the Cross Creek trail. I fired, and I hit him. I know because he staggered and then ran off. I reloaded, but he was gone. I thought he'd crawled away and died, but obviously, he didn't. Looking at him, though, he should have... a smaller man would have... But never mind," he said brightly. "No harm, no foul. I have him now, and I can finish the job."

How long had he been lying on my porch, I wonder?

"You killed Julie, didn't you?" she whispered.

He sucked in a breath through his teeth, making a hissing sound. "That was unfortunate," he said. "Your niece was a tall girl. I saw her at the Red Grove North trailhead, not far from my cabin. She was wearing the same jacket Zach was wearing when he shouted at me. It was overcast, dark under the trees. I thought she was him. I had this with me." He lifted the pistol from his lap and then let it rest on his knee again.

She said she was going to hike Red Grove East, Mallory thought. *Why did she change her mind?*

"I couldn't believe how lucky I was," he continued. "There was no one around. The place was deserted, as it usually is. I shot her three times. Then I saw the dog. I shot at it, but I missed and it ran away. Then I realized what I'd done. It was a stupid mistake, but..." He shrugged. "What can you do? I shoved her body in the Bronco and drove to the cabin and—"

"And you buried her body and drove her Bronco to Maryville, where you dumped it behind a strip mall," Mallory finished for him. "Well, we found it this morning at a scrap yard, and the sheriff's sent a truck to recover it. They'll know it was you. They'll find something; they always do."

"Hah! Good luck with that," Wilson said, smiling. "I wore gloves, and even if they do, Cundiff will have to cover for me. He owes me big time."

"You mean," she said as she suddenly realized, "you know about the sheriff and his—"

"Who do you think subsidizes his family operations?" Wilson laughed. "Not me personally, of course. But the Burns family, the Alexanders, the Lawrys; they all have their fingers in all sorts of pies around here. Cundiff might make money moving things, but he works for Carmichael Burns."

No wonder Cundiff didn't want to investigate Julie's disappearance, Mallory thought. *Somehow I've got to get out of this mess.*

"Well, here we are," Wilson said. "Take a right at the mailbox and stop in front of the cabin."

Mallory pulled the truck gently to a stop so as to not spook the man with the gun.

"Now get out slowly," he said. "And leave the door open."

She did as she was instructed, knowing that this was the moment she might be able to make a break for it and lose the doctor in the woods.

But I can't leave Zach behind to die.

No, she wouldn't do that. She decided to bide her time

CHAPTER 28

and hope she could find an opportunity to save them both. Unfortunately, that decision was made for her.

Wilson opened his door and slid out carefully. "You've done fine so far, Mallory," he said. "Last chance. I'd love to keep you around a little longer," he continued as he walked slowly around the back of the truck, the gun pointed at Zach. "What do you say? You want to stay and play. I'd make it worth your while and, of course... you'd live," he finished with an evil smile.

She had no idea how to answer him. She knew she had to try to persuade him she wouldn't try to kill him the first chance she got. But then...

"Hmm," he said and sucked in a breath through his teeth, shaking his head. "Too late, Mallory. Even in the dark, the look on your face tells me everything. Oh, well. Never mind."

He glanced into the pickup bed, aimed, and pulled the trigger.

"NOOOO!" Mallory screamed.

29

MONDAY EVENING 8PM

Tucker Randall made good time until he made the turn off Highway 64 and headed toward Greasy Creek and then Kimsey Mountain Highway.

"Highway," he muttered as he negotiated the narrow, heavily forested, two-lane up the mountain. "What a frickin' joke that is."

It was the first time he'd driven this route, and he didn't know the area. He didn't know if there were deer on the road. And, even though it was only just after eight o'clock, and it was still light, he had to have his headlights on. It was a thirty-mile-an-hour road and he was doing sixty, and he'd had his teeth gritted all the way, so much so his jaw was aching. He took the bends too fast, almost losing control twice. He even passed a red car on one of the bends, gritting his teeth and half-closing his eyes as he did so. *How far ahead can they be?* he wondered as he fishtailed another tight bend. *Whoa! There it is... I think.*

He almost missed the turn. He slammed on the brakes and went skidding to a stop, tires screeching.

He backed up a little and checked the mailbox. *Yes! This is it,* he thought as he hauled down hard on the wheel and made a right onto the narrow dirt track.

Come on... come on, come on, he thought savagely as he negotiated the track and the overhanging tree limbs, branches brushing both sides of his SUV. And all the while, just one thought was running through his mind. *Please let me get there before he kills her,* over and over.

He crested a rise, entered a small clearing, and there it was, Mallory's pickup, directly in front of him. He hit the brakes and skidded to a stop just as a gunshot rang out. "No!" he shouted as he pushed the car door open and jumped out—just in time to hear a second gunshot. Without pausing to think, he yanked the Glock from his shoulder holster and ran forward.

"Well, lookie here," he heard a voice call out. "By all the luck in the stars. Tucker Randall. How fortuitous."

"It's all over, doctor," Tucker called back. "I know what you did."

"Hah. You do, huh? No one will believe you." Wilson laughed. "I'm a lauded member of the community. I'm a generous doctor with a rich family. And the sheriff's covering for me. And you, you're just a two-bit hack who likes seeing himself on television—"

"And you're a frickin' psycho. Let, me, go, you monster," he heard Mallory shout.

Tucker blew out a breath to steady himself. *Whew! Thank God. She's still alive. The sheriff? What the hell?*

"I called the state police," Tucker shouted. "They're on their way," Tucker lied.

"You're full of shit, Randall," Wilson shouted. "I don't

believe you. Now, if you want this little bitch to live, step forward, slowly."

"I have a gun, and it's pointed right at you," Tucker shouted. "Let her go and give yourself up."

"That's not going to happen. I also have a gun, and it's pointed at her pretty little head. Now step forward where I can see you or I'll blow her brains out."

"Shoot him, Tucker," Mallory yelled. "Shoot the crazy son of a bitch."

"Now, now, Mallory," Wilson said mildly. "There's no need for that kind of language. I said come forward, Randall. If you don't, I swear I'll shoot her in the head."

Cautiously, Tucker walked slowly forward until he could see Wilson with Mallory in front of him, his arm around her neck and a gun at her ear.

"Drop your gun, Randall."

"So you can shoot me?" Randall replied, his Glock aimed at what little he could see of the doctor. "I don't think so. No matter what you do next, you're done. You're not going to get away with it."

"You think?" he snapped. "With you two out of the way, who's to know?"

"I told you, the state troopers are on their way," Tucker lied, waiting for an opening. "I told them where the bodies are buried."

Wilson frowned, looked worried for a moment, then said, "Bullshit! As I said, I don't believe you. Now drop the gun or—"

He was interrupted by the sound of an engine. Tucker resisted the urge to turn, but then headlights cut through the dusk, lighting up Mallory's truck and the two figures in front of it.

"Who's that?" Wilson yelled. "Who did you bring with you?"

"I didn't bring anybody," Tucker replied.

The car pulled up beside his SUV. He glanced to his left. It was red, a red Honda Civic. *That's the car I passed on the way up here. It's Linda. What the hell?*

The car door opened, and she stepped out and shouted, "John? John, what are you doing? Have you gone mad?"

"Linnie? What the hell are you doing here?" Wilson shouted. "Go away."

"John, why are you doing this?" she asked. "And where did you get that gun?"

Wilson took the gun away from Mallory's ear and swept it back and forth, pointing it first at Linda, then at Tucker.

Tucker decided enough was enough. He fired a shot low and to the left, hoping to distract Wilson.

Mallory's driver's side front tire exploded. Wilson jerked, startled by the unexpected bang just to his right, and Mallory exploded into action. She grabbed Wilson's wrist with both hands, ripped it away from her throat, spun around, whipped his arm up and over her head, spun around again and slammed her forearm down on the back of the doctor's left elbow as hard as she could. Even in the echoes of the gunshot, Tucker heard the crunch of broken bone. He couldn't believe how quickly Mallory had moved.

Wilson dropped his gun and screamed. "AAAHHH. Oh crap oh crap oh crap. You broke my arm. You stupid bitch. You broke my fricking arm. Ugh!" He gasped as Mallory landed a vicious kick to his ribs, and he crumpled forward and fell to the ground.

"Mallory, stop!" Tucker yelled as she reared back for another kick. "We need him alive."

"No, we don't," she yelled as her foot slammed into the doctor's chest again.

Tucker holstered his weapon, ran forward, and grabbed

her before she could land another blow. "Mallory, it's over. We did it," he said.

"We didn't do anything, Tucker," she snapped. He could see the tears rolling down her cheeks. "He killed Julie. He killed Zach. He killed Zach's mother."

Tucker pulled her close as she began to sob uncontrollably. "I know, Mallory. I know."

He looked around and saw Linda Warner on her knees beside Wilson.

"Why did you do this, John?" she asked as he moaned in pain. "Why did you kidnap that girl? How could you? You're a doctor."

"Just covering other people's mistakes," he mumbled. "Can't trust anyone anymore."

"But I thought you trusted me," she whispered. "I thought you loved me."

The doctor half choked, half laughed, and then gasped. "Are you serious, you stupid… OW," he yelped as she punched his broken elbow.

Tucker heaved a deep breath, kicked Wilson's gun under Mallory's truck, then took out his phone and called 911.

"9-1-1, what's your emergency?"

"This is Tucker Randall," he said. "I'm a private investigator. I'm at a house on Kimsey Mountain Road. I need an ambulance, the state police—not the sheriff's department—and a cadaver dog unit." He gave her the full address and then waited for her response.

"You have a victim in need of medical attention. You also need the state police and a K-9 unit. Please confirm."

"No, not a victim," Tucker corrected. "A criminal."

"Message received and understood. Dispatching units to your location. Please stay on the line."

"He was right," Mallory said. "You didn't call the state police, did you?"

"Nope. I didn't," he said as he steered her toward the cabin. "Where's Zach Burns? I heard you say Wilson killed him."

"He's in the back of the truck," she replied, her voice breaking. "Wilson shot him just as you arrived."

"Are you sure he's dead?" Tucker asked.

"I think so. I think he shot him in the head."

"I'd better take a look," Tucker said. "Stay here."

He was back almost immediately. "Yes. He's dead. There's a bullet wound in his forehead. I'm sorry you had to witness that."

"I would have tried to get the gun away from him sooner, but I just didn't have an opportunity." Mallory sniffed. "Julie's dead, Tucker. He told me he killed her. I think she's here somewhere."

"If she is, they'll find her," Tucker said.

His phone crackled. "Are you there, Mr. Randall?"

"Yes, I'm here."

"The state police are on their way. ETA, seventeen minutes. How are things where you are?"

"Under control," Tucker replied.

"Thank you. Stay on the line please."

"Why did you blow out my tire?" Mallory said.

"Sorry," Tucker said. "I was trying to distract him."

"Well, you did. Thank you."

Tucker looked around the door of the cabin for a spare key but couldn't find one.

"Linda," he called. "Is there a key anywhere?"

"I'll get it," she said as she stood up and left the doctor's side.

She reached up and felt along the top of the picture window and found the key to a lock on a small garden

CHAPTER 29

shed. She went inside and retrieved the house key from under an old gas can.

Once inside the cabin, Mallory began pacing back and forth, a bundle of nervous energy.

"I'm really sorry, Mallory—" Tucker began.

But she waved him off. "I'm glad it's over," was all she said. And then continued pacing, her arms wrapped around herself, staring off into space.

Tucker inwardly shook his head. It had been a terrible ordeal with an explosive climax, literally. And he was dreading making the call to Jennifer and Jared Romero. At least they'd found Julie... or soon would. Mallory, he knew, would insist on being present for the removal of Julie's remains, and the pain would tear her apart.

Tucker sat down on the couch in the living room to wait for the state police. He was quietly content, knowing that he'd arrived just in time to save Mallory, though unfortunately not Zach; but, as he looked around, he frowned. Something was bothering him. He had the feeling he'd been in the room before, but he knew he hadn't. He looked around again, then stood up, looked around again, and then it clicked. He pursed his lips, looked down at the rug, dropped to one knee and pulled back the corner of the rug to reveal a large, dark stain on the wood floor.

"What is that?" Mallory asked as she stepped to his side, her arms folded over her chest. "That's weird," she said. "It looks like... is that blood?"

"I think it must be where Wynona Burns was killed," he said. "I recognize the room from the crime scene photos; the rug, the pictures."

"He cut her throat," Mallory said. "He told me about it. She got pregnant. He didn't want that."

"I wish... I wish I could have done something more," Tucker said with a sigh as he dropped the rug back in place and stood up. "I feel like I haven't accomplished… anything."

"There's nothing more you could have done. Julie was already dead when Jen hired you. Now we know where she is. Without you, we wouldn't be here now. You saved my life, Tucker. I'm still here only because of you. Thank you."

"You don't need to thank me," Tucker replied.

He looked around the room again, then said, "This isn't just where he brought his dates. It's where he brought his victims: Wynona, Zach, Julie and… you, and… maybe they'll find more bodies out there." He stared out the window and then continued, "He brought you and Zach here to kill you… You know, Linda said he seemed happy here."

"Maybe this was the only place he ever felt fully in control," Mallory whispered. "Bad marriage, endless patient problems…"

"A failing practice," Tucker added, "one affair after another." He sighed. "But this isn't how I thought it would end."

"They're coming," Mallory said. "I can hear the sirens."

"I hear them, too," Tucker said. "It's time. Come on. Let's go."

And they stepped out into the flashing lights.

EPILOGUE

SIX MONTHS LATER

Mallory Carver was seated in the front row of the courtroom alongside her sister Jennifer, Jared, their daughter Katie, and her husband. Their son Justin and his wife Jackie were seated in the row behind. Tucker Randall and Linda Warner were seated together two rows back.

It had been a while since Mallory had last seen Tucker, and it made her happy to see him now, even if it was under such stressful circumstances.

Judge Andrew Grayson, something of a fixture in the local judiciary system, was a tough, no-nonsense old bird known for his harsh sentences. The trial was over, and all that was left was the sentencing.

The judge nodded to the bailiff, then fixed his beady eyes on the defense table.

"The defendant will rise," the bailiff called.

The doctor and his defense team rose to their feet.

"John Robert Wilson, having been found guilty on all charges. On count one, that you did willfully murder

Wynona Iris Burns, I hereby sentence you to prison for the rest of your life. On count two..." and so it went on until the doctor had accrued three life sentences plus fifty years, all to run consecutively and without the possibility of parole.

And for the first time in seven months, Mallory breathed her first truly free breath. "It's really over, isn't it?" she asked Jen.

Jen smiled at her and said, "Yes, it's over."

"I should have figured it out sooner," Mallory said. "I could have—"

"You did everything you could. More than I ever thought possible," Jen said, wrapping her arms around her. "It's not your fault. You... You and Mr. Randall, you found her, and that's all that matters. We were able to bring her home. Thank you, Mallory."

But the truth was, Mallory Carver couldn't get over the fact that she didn't notice Julie drifting away from her or how, knowing Kal Cundiff as well as she did, she never knew about the Cundiff family's nefarious operations.

Neither Kal nor his father, nor any member of the family had been charged with anything. The only evidence against them was the stories Tucker and Mallory told the state police, but as Tucker had known all along, it was all hearsay, and the powerful Burns, Alexander and Lawry families closed ranks, and the stories were officially deemed the stuff of urban legend. In other words, they got away with it.

So, Mallory thought, *I guess I'll just have to believe that we did everything we could.*

Finally, after the court cleared, Mallory wished her sister well and walked slowly out into the lobby, where she bumped into Tucker, who was talking to Linda Warner.

"So, *Mr. Randall,* Mrs. Warner. How are you both?" she

EPILOGUE

asked. "How's the latest case going? How d'you like working for Tucker?"

"Hah!" Tucker said. "You haven't changed a bit, Mallory. Still with the questions." He smiled at her, stepped forward and gave her a quick hug. "It's so nice to see you again. How've you been?"

"I asked first," Mallory said. "How are you two getting along?"

Linda rolled her eyes. "He's fine. He misses you. Talks about you all the time."

"No, I don't," he snapped.

"Yes, you do. Why only yest—"

"That's enough, Linda," he said, smiling.

"As to your query, yes, I'm fine... except for my back. I think I need to see a chiropractor and—"

"Oh, I know someone," Mallory said. "Jemma Moon, occupational injury and massage therapist. Do you want her card?"

Tucker looked uncomfortable. "Um... Mallory. No! After what happened last time. No thank you. No offense, but I think I'll find one for myself if you don't mind."

"Oh, come on," Mallory retorted. "That was—"

"Yes, I know," Tucker said, interrupting her. "Well, it was nice to see you again. I, that is we, need to be going. Linda?"

"Just a minute, sir," Linda said. "I need a quick word with Mallory."

"I'll be outside. Look after yourself, Mallory. Call me if you need me," Tucker said, then turned and walked away.

"He really is spooked, isn't he?" Mallory asked.

"Not as much as he puts on, I think," Linda said with a smile. "Well, are you ready for tomorrow?"

Mallory couldn't hide her smirk. "You bet I am."

By eight-thirty the following morning, Tucker was in his office, ready to peruse his list of potential cases.

He'd taken a long, hot shower, dressed in tan pants and a white shirt—open neck, no tie—eaten a light breakfast of two scrambled eggs on toast, drank two cups of coffee and then went to his office to find Linda was already there, as she had been for the last five months. *She's been a miracle,* Tucker thought.

When Debbie left, he didn't think he'd find anybody to replace her, not so quickly, anyway. But there Linda was, no job, highly experienced and needing work, so he'd hired her on the spot.

He spent a half-hour looking at the half-dozen files Linda had left for him the day before. *A missing show dog in Indiana worth $15,000? Hmm, interesting. A stolen Mercedes; pass. A possible affair in Ohio; well, he's worth enough, and if she wins...*

Linda popped her head in the doorway. "Mr. Randall? D'you have a minute, please?"

"Sure, come on in. Sit down. What's up?"

"I'm afraid I'm going to have to leave you."

"What?" he said, his head snapping up to look at her. "Oh no. Look, if you need a vacation or something—"

"Uh-uh," she said, shaking her head. "I was happy to help out for a little while," she explained, "but this isn't what I want to be doing anymore. It reminds me of... well, you know."

I know all too well! "Wow, this is... sudden. Are you giving me a two-week notice? I suppose I'd better put out an ad or something."

"Oh, I already did that, sir. And I've already interviewed my replacement. She's a real go-getter, very organized, and # EPILOGUE

likes to be involved. I think you'll find she's just what you're looking for."

"You did, huh?" Tucker replied skeptically, and then it began to dawn on him. "Now wait a—"

"I've already explained the job to her in detail," Linda continued, "and I'm certain you'll find her to be well-qualified."

"You must think I'm—" The door opened. "Oh no," he said.

Mallory stepped into the office, smiling widely, and sat down next to Linda. She was wearing a blouse and skirt, and her hair was piled up on top of her head in a way he hadn't seen before.

Tucker heaved a huge sigh, leaned back in his chair, shook his head, and gave up. He knew when he was beaten.

"Good morning, *Ms. Carver*," he said dryly, thinking she was so dressed up she barely looked like herself.

"Mornin', *Tuck*," she said with an impish smile. "How's my timing, Linda?"

"About ten seconds late, but acceptable," Linda replied.

"So you two cooked this thing up between you?" Tucker asked. "But why? All you had to do was ask for the job."

The two women shared a glance and smirked. "And I'm sure you mean that, sir," Linda said. "And I'm really pleased, for the both of you, but no. No notice. Ms. Carver, as you call her, can start today. I do have something waiting for me. I have a date at noon."

"Ooh, with who?" Mallory asked. "Or should I say, whom?" she asked, lifting her chin and smiling at Tucker.

"Excuse me?" Tucker said. "Aren't we forgetting that you two conspired to cut me out of the hiring decision for my own business?"

"And can you think of a single reason why you shouldn't hire me?" Mallory asked.

"Oh, I can think of several reasons—" he retorted. But then he looked at her. She had a new confidence about her, and her eyes were smiling at him.

"Oh, hell," he said. "Okay, but I can't have you going around dressed like that. You'll scare the clients to death. The top's fine, but if you're going to accompany me out in the field, you'll need to wear pants and not those damn skinny things."

Mallory cocked an eyebrow. "Out in the field, *sir?* I thought I was going to be your secretary."

"Oh come on, Mallory," he said. "If you think, that I think, that you're going to sit in here while I'm out in the field, then you must also think that I'm as stupid as I look."

Linda laughed. "Well, on that note," Linda said and stood up, "if you'll excuse me, I need to head home and put on something entirely inappropriate. I want to see if I can make Howard O'Neal's eyes pop out."

"Howard O—" Mallory looked confused for a moment and then, "Wait! You mean *Howie?*"

"What can I say?" Linda shrugged. "I met him at that horrible bar where you used to work. He's been lonely a long time. And we... sort of clicked." She tossed her head and said, "Well, ta-ta, then. Don't you two do anything I wouldn't do... Oh no. Ignore that. There's nothing I wouldn't do." And with a big smile, Linda swept out of the office.

Tucker sighed. "Geez," he said, shaking his head. "So when did you two get together to cook this up?"

"Actually, about five months ago," Mallory said. "I would have started earlier, but I needed to take care of a few things first. I had to make arrangements for my house and generally help Jen through the worst time of her life. But I'm ready now."

EPILOGUE

"What do you mean, arrangements for your house?" Tucker asked.

"Katie's pregnant, and she wanted to move back here. And since I was taking this fabulous new job, I sublet my house to her."

Tucker frowned. "Why not just let her live there?"

"Would *you* do anything like that without getting it in writing? Which reminds me, here's my application."

She handed over the forms Linda had supplied. They were neatly filled out and impressive. Tucker nodded his head from side to side as he glanced through them, then put them away in his desk drawer.

"I can file those for you if you like," she said with that same impish smile on her lips and in her eyes.

"Later," Tucker said dryly. "You can do it later. Right now, we have work to do. If I'm going to be able to pay you, I need to find our next case… By the way, how much did Linda offer you?"

She opened her clutch, took out a piece of paper and slid it across the desk to him.

He glanced at it, then at her, and said, "Wow, you'd better be worth it."

"Oh, I am," she replied. "Now, about *our* next case," Mallory said with a smile. "I think you should skip to the bottom of the pile and look at the one about the coal mine sabotage in West Virginia."

"Why would I want to go to West Virginia?" Tucker asked.

"Take a look," Mallory insisted.

And as Tucker read the file, he realized it was just the kind of case he liked, a real David versus Goliath story, a large corporation trying to squeeze a competitor out.

"Okay," he said. "I'll give you a try. We'll see how you work out."

"I usually begin my workout with a five-mile run, then a couple of dozen seventy-pound bench presses, followed by a dozen fifty-pound squats," Mallory replied.

Tucker couldn't help but laugh. *Oh, this is going to change everything,* he thought. *But maybe change is exactly what I need.*

"Very well. Go ahead and give West Virginia a call," he said, smiling at her, "and tell them Randall and Carver are on the case."

Thank you so much for reading, Never Say Dead, the first book in the Randall & Carver Mysteries series. I hope you enjoyed it!

If you did, you'll love the sequel, Happily Never After.

Turn the page for a preview of this second book in the series.

HAPPILY NEVER AFTER

RANDALL & CARVER MYSTERIES

BOOK TWO

By

Blair Howard

PROLOGUE

WHO KILLED FRANNY MCNEER?

Extract from Thomas Drews' podcast dated March 15, 2022: *Who Killed Franny McNeer?*

…assuming Luthor McNeer didn't kill his wife as he has always claimed, we must substitute "It" for "He" or "She" when referencing the killer. And I must warn you, I take a little literary license in my narrative.

At almost midnight on the evening of Friday, July 8, 2016, the killer crept into the McNeer bedroom. Franny McNeer was asleep, alone, in the marital bed, snoring softly, perhaps even dreaming.

The killer stood for a moment in the light of the full moon, staring down at her, knife in hand, then stepped around the bed, took a deep breath, raised the knife and plunged it through the covers into the sleeping woman's breast, and then withdrew it and plunged it again and again and again into Franny's body, each blow more savage than the one before until the killer, exhausted by its efforts, stepped away, blood dripping from the knife blade. Franny McNeer died quickly. Nineteen of the forty-three stab wounds would have been fatal; this according to Dr. Sheddon, the Hamilton County Chief Medical Examiner. An act of rage, he called it, and rage it must have been for her assailant to stab her so many times.

We know from the bloody footprints that, eventually, the killer took a step back, and the knife, slippery with blood, slid from its fingers and fell to the floor. The killer then turned away and walked quickly and silently from the room, leaving a trail of bloody footprints on the carpet. Franny McNeer, her eyes wide, stared sightlessly up at the ceiling.

Two days later, Luthor McNeer, Franny's husband, was arrested and charged with her murder. It was Luthor who discovered his wife's body. He claimed to have been asleep downstairs on the couch in the living room when something disturbed him and he went upstairs and found her in their blood-soaked bed. He immediately went to her and held her in his arms, but it was too late.

Luthor, now with blood on his clothes and his shoes, called the emergency services and was found standing beside the bed. Of course, he claimed he had nothing to do with her death, but his was the only DNA found at the scene, and there were no signs of an intruder, even though Luthor swore all the doors and windows were locked. The knife handle, slick with the victim's blood, was devoid of fingerprints.

Was Luthor McNeer asleep on the couch as he claims? Was it an intruder that brutally murdered Franny McNeer? In either case, the police didn't think so, and Luthor had no explanation as to why he'd slept through the horrific murder. He denied he was drunk, and blood analysis proved it to be true. Nor were there drugs in his system. So how could he have slept through it all? Luthor himself has no explanation.

Luthor was tried for his wife's murder and was found guilty and sentenced to twenty-five years to life imprisonment. He always claimed he was innocent. But if it wasn't him... who did kill Franny McNeer, and why?

1

MONDAY, NOVEMBER 18, 2024

8am

"Annie, will you please get yourself in here?" Mallory shouted.

The dog stopped its sniffing, turned and gave her a look of disdain. Rarely did Mallory raise her voice to the Border Collie, but it was eight-thirty on a Monday morning in November. It was cold and drizzling with rain outside, and Mallory was not looking forward to the week ahead. Work of late had been, well, boring. A long-running financial investigation—one of Tucker's many fortes—three nasty divorce cases and a missing person case, only the person wasn't missing at all. She'd simply taken an unannounced leave of absence and had checked herself into a Benedictine convent for a month to "Find my inner self." Even so, it had taken all of Tucker's many skills to track her down, whereupon she'd told him in no uncertain terms to F off and leave her alone with the nuns.

Mallory, a one-time-bartender with a penchant for organization and true crime podcasts, had joined Tucker Randall's one-man organization almost a year earlier after he solved the disappearance of her beloved niece, Julie, with unwavering help from Mallory. Unfortunately, though, the investigation ended in tragedy when it was discovered that Julie had been murdered by Dr. John Williams, a local family GP.

Jennifer Romero, Mallory's older sister and Julie's mother, had hired Tucker, an ex-FBI special agent and something of a loner, to find her missing daughter. Mallory had, much to Tucker's chagrin, insisted on sticking her nose in. At first, he wanted nothing to do with Mallory or her in-depth research. But, as the case wore on, and Tucker, unused to the great outdoors, began to flounder and soon realized that Mallory was much more than the ditsy bartender he'd thought her to be. Thus was born an unusual alliance between the two, and, when the case was brought to its tragic conclusion, he offered her a job as a kind of junior partner. Little did he know what he was letting himself in for.

"Annie," Mallory snapped at the dog, her eyes narrowed, "if you don't come inside right now..." She let the threat dangle unfinished. Annie, smarter even than the average Border Collie, got the message and slunk past her into the office and over to her bed, where she sat down and stared defiantly at her mistress.

"I swear you get worse by the day," she muttered, then went to the door that opened into Randall's home, opened it and yelled, "TUCKER, are you coming, or what?" Then she turned away and went to her desk and sat down.

"Geez, what is wrong with you?" Tucker said as he

CHAPTER 1

walked through the door, his jacket over his arm. "You have a rough weekend or something?"

"No," she replied, "but we need to talk. We're hemorrhaging money, and these stupid divorce cases aren't helping. We need something more... meaty. Something we can get our teeth into. Something with a decent paycheck."

"Something *I* can get my teeth into, you mean," he replied with a grin.

"Oh, dear Lord," she said, rolling her eyes. "I'm doing all the work as it is and..." She paused, gave him a grossly exaggerated frown, and then continued. "Speaking of that. Isn't it time you gave me a raise?"

He made a face, shook his head and said, "And what would I pay you with? You just said we're... How did you put it? Oh, yes, hemorrhaging money." He grinned at her triumphantly.

She smiled sweetly at him and said, "How about from that rainy-day account you failed to tell me about?"

"But it's not raining—"

"Oh, yes, it is," she said. "Go outside and look."

"That's not what I meant, and you know it," he said, then sat down in the guest chair in front of his desk. "But you're right. We do need something to pump a little life into things, even if it means we have to travel. There's this thing we've been dodging in Shreveport; well, you've been dodging it."

"Tucker, there has to be plenty to do around here without us having to go gallivanting off into the bayous. Don't you think?"

"I'd hardly call Shreveport bayou country," he retorted. "And, if there's plenty to do around here, as you say, why aren't we getting any of it?"

"Because you're old-fashioned and won't let me do some marketing."

"Marketing? What do you know about marketing?"

"I know if people don't know you're here, they can't hire you," she said.

"So what do you suggest?" he asked, crossing his legs and folding his arms.

"I suggest we hire a marketing company to get our name out there. I've been doing some research... and don't look at me like that. Stop grinning at me, too. You look like... You look silly. Anyway, I found two companies I think might do a good job. What do you think?"

"I think..." he said and paused, smiling at her, "that if I don't let you do as you please, you'll make my life hell. So go ahead and look into it. But do *not* spend any money without checking with me first. Understood?"

"Understood," she replied. "Now, how about that raise?"

"Forget it," he said, uncrossing his legs and rising to his feet when the phone rang.

"Randall and Carver," Mallory said. "How can I help you?"

"Mallory, is that you?"

Mallory frowned. "Vinnie?"

Like what you have read so far? Get the full book now.

Did you know you can get signed paperbacks of all of Blair Howards Books at www.blairhowardbooks.com.

FROM BLAIR HOWARD

The Harry Starke Genesis Series
8 Books in Series as of 2024

The Harry Starke Series
24 Books in Series as of 2024

The Lt. Kate Gazzara Murder Files
20 Books in Series as of 2024

Randall And Carver Mysteries
2 Books in Series as of 2024

The Peacemaker Series
3 Books in Series as of 2024

The O'Sullivan Chronicles: Civil War Series
5 Books in Series as of 2024

FROM BLAIR C. HOWARD

The Sovereign Star Series
7 Books in Series as of 2024

ABOUT THE AUTHOR

Blair Howard is a retired journalist turned novelist. He's the author of more than 50 novels including the international best-selling Harry Starke series of detective crime stories, the Lt. Kate Gazzara Police Procedural series, the Harry Starke Genesis series, and the Randall & Carver Mysteries. He's also the author of the Peacemaker series of international spy thrillers and five Civil War/Western novels.

If you enjoy reading Science Fiction thrillers, Mr. Howard has made his debut into the genre with, The Sovereign Stars Series under the name, Blair C. Howard.

www.BlairHowardBooks.com

Made in United States
North Haven, CT
21 April 2025